Also by Barbara O'Connor

Beethoven in Paradise

Me and Rupert Goody

Moonpie and Ivy

Fame and Glory in Freedom, Georgia

Taking Care of Moses

How to Steal a Dog

Greetings from Nowhere

The Small Adventure of Popeye and Elvis

The Fantastic Secret of Owen Jester

On the Road to Mr. Mineo's

Barbara O'Connor

Wish

SQUARE
FISH

FARRAR STRAUS GIROUX / *New York*

Special thanks to Barbara and Harvey Markowitz, for always being there ... and
to Kirby Larson, Sue Hill Long, and Augusta Scattergood. Long live the sisterhood.

**SQUARE
FISH**

An imprint of Macmillan Publishing Group, LLC
120 Broadway, New York, NY 10271
mackids.com

Square Fish and the Square Fish logo are trademarks of Macmillan and
are used by Farrar Straus Giroux under license from Macmillan.

Our books may be purchased in bulk for promotional, educational, or business
use. Please contact your local bookseller or the Macmillan Corporate and
Premium Sales Department at (800) 221-7945 ext. 5442 or by
email at MacmillanSpecialMarkets@macmillan.com.

Library of Congress Cataloging-in-Publication Data

Names: O'Connor, Barbara, author.
Title: Wish / Barbara O'Connor.
Description: New York : Farrar Straus Giroux, 2016. | Summary: "A story about
   a girl who, with the help of the dog of her dreams, discovers that family doesn't always
   have to be related—they are simply people who love you for who you are"—Provided
   by publisher.
Identifiers: LCCN 2015034459 | ISBN 978-1-250-14405-8 (paperback)
   ISBN 978-0-374-30275-7 (ebook)
Subjects: | CYAC: Human-animal relationships—Fiction. | Dogs—Fiction. |
   Families—Fiction. | Conduct of life—Fiction. | BISAC: JUVENILE FICTION /
   Animals / Dogs. | JUVENILE FICTION / Family / General (see also headings
   under Social Issues). | JUVENILE FICTION / Social Issues / Friendship.
Classification: LCC PZ7.O217 Wi 2016 | DDC [Fic]—dc23
LC record available at http://lccn.loc.gov/2015034459

Originally published in the United States by Farrar Straus Giroux
First Square Fish edition, 2017
Square Fish logo designed by Filomena Tuosto

AR: 5.0 / LEXILE: 850L

For Monika,
true friend

Wish

One

I looked down at the paper on my desk.

The "Getting to Know You" paper.

At the top, Mrs. Willibey had written "Charlemagne Reese."

I put a big X over *Charlemagne* and wrote "Charlie."

My name is Charlie. Charlemagne is a dumb name for a girl and I have told my mama that about a gazillion times.

I looked around me at all the hillbilly kids doing math in their workbooks.

My best friend, Alvina, told me they would be hillbilly kids.

"You will hate it in Colby," she said. "There's just red dirt roads and hillbilly kids there." She had flipped her silky hair over her shoulder and added, "I bet they eat squirrels."

I glanced at the lunch boxes under the desks around me and wondered if there were any squirrel sandwiches in them.

I looked back down at the paper in front of me. I was supposed to fill in all this stuff so my new teacher could get to know me.

On the line beside *Describe your family*, I wrote, "Bad."

What is your favorite subject in school? "None."

List three of your favorite activities. "Soccer, ballet, and fighting."

Two of those favorite activities were lies but one of them was the truth.

I am fond of fighting.

My sister, Jackie, inherited Daddy's inky black hair and I inherited his fiery red temper. If I had a nickel for every time I've heard "The apple don't fall far from the tree," I'd be rich. Daddy fights so much that everybody calls him Scrappy. In fact, at this very minute, while I'm stuck here in Colby, North Carolina, surrounded by hillbilly kids, ole Scrappy is back in Raleigh in the county jail again because of his fondness for fighting.

And I don't need a crystal ball to know that at this very minute, in our house in Raleigh, smack-dab in the middle of the day, Mama is in bed with the curtains drawn and empty soda cans on the nightstand. She will stay in that bed the livelong day. If I was there, she wouldn't care one little bit if I went to school or stayed on the couch watching TV and eating cookies for lunch.

"But that's just the tip of the iceberg," that social services lady said when she rattled off a list of reasons why I was getting shipped off to this sorry excuse for a town to live with two people I didn't even know. "It's better to stay with kin," she told me. "Gus and Bertha are kin."

"What kind of kin?" I asked.

She explained how Bertha is Mama's sister and Gus is her husband. She said they didn't have any kids and they were happy to take me in.

"Then how come Jackie gets to stay with Carol Lee?" I asked about a million times. Carol Lee is Jackie's best friend. She lives in a fancy brick house with a swimming pool. Her mama gets out of bed every morning and her daddy is not called Scrappy.

So that lady told me again how Jackie was practically a grownup and would be graduating from high school in a couple of months.

When I pointed out that I was in fifth grade and not exactly a baby, she sighed and smiled a fake smile and said, "Charlie, you have to live with Gus and Bertha for a while."

I'd never laid eyes on those people and now I was supposed to *live* with them? When I asked how long I had to be there, she said until things settled down and Mama got her feet on the ground.

Well, how hard is it to put your dang feet on the ground? is what I thought about that.

"You need a stable family environment," she told me. But I knew what she really meant was, "You need a family that's not all broken like yours is."

Still, I whined and argued and whined and argued, but here I am in Colby, North Carolina, staring down at this "Getting to Know You" paper.

"Have you finished, Charlemagne?" Mrs. Willibey was suddenly beside me.

"My name is Charlie," I said, and a greasy-haired boy in the front of the class let out a sputtering laugh. I sent one of my famous glares his way till he hushed up and turned red.

I handed Mrs. Willibey that paper and watched her eyes dart back and forth as she read it. Her neck got splotchy red and the corners of her mouth twitched. She didn't even look at me before she marched back up to the front of the room and dropped that paper on her desk like it was a hot potato.

I slumped down in my seat and wiped my sweaty palms on my shorts. It was only April, but it was already hot as blazes.

"You want me to help you with that?" The boy in front of me pointed at the math worksheet on my desk. He had red hair and wore ugly black glasses.

"No," I said.

He shrugged, took a pencil out of his desk, and headed to the pencil sharpener.

Up.

Down.

Up.

Down.

That's how he walked.

Like one leg was shorter than the other.

And he dragged one foot along the floor, so his sneaker made squeaking noises.

I glanced at the clock.

Dang it! I had missed 11:11.

I have a list of all the ways there are to make a wish,

7

like seeing a white horse or blowing a dandelion. Looking at a clock at exactly 11:11 is on my list. I'd learned that from some old man who owned the bait and tackle shop out by the lake where Scrappy and I used to go fishing. Now that I'd missed 11:11, I was going to have to find another way to get in my wish for the day. I hadn't missed one single day of making my wish since the end of fourth grade, so I sure didn't want to miss one now.

Then Mrs. Willibey nodded toward that redheaded boy sharpening his pencil and said, "Howard, why don't you be Charlie's Backpack Buddy for a while?"

Mrs. Willibey explained that when a new kid comes to school, their Backpack Buddy shows them around and tells them the rules till they get settled.

Howard grinned and said, "Yes, ma'am," and that was that. I had a Backpack Buddy whether I wanted one or not.

The rest of the afternoon creeped along so slow I couldn't hardly stand it. I stared out the window while kids took turns bragging about their social studies projects. A misty rain had begun to fall and dark gray clouds hovered over the tops of the mountains in the distance.

When the bell finally rang, I hightailed it out of there and headed for the bus. I hurried up the aisle and dropped into the last row. I kept my eyes on a piece of dried-up chewing gum stuck to the seat in front of me while I sent laser thoughts zipping and zapping around the bus.

Do not sit next to me.

Do not sit next to me.

Do not sit next to me.

If I had to be stuck on a bus full of kids I didn't even know, I wanted to at least sit by myself.

My laser thoughts seemed to be working, so I took my eyes off of the gum and glanced out the window.

That redheaded boy with the up-down walk was hurrying toward the bus, his backpack bouncing against him with every step.

When he got on the bus, I quickly looked back at the gum and sent my laser thoughts out again.

But that boy didn't waste a minute shuffling up the aisle and plopping himself right down next to me.

Then he thrust his hand out at me and said, "Hey. I'm Howard Odom." He pushed at his ugly black glasses and added, "Your Backpack Buddy."

Now, what kind of kid shakes hands like that? No kid I ever knew.

He kept his hand there and stared me down till I couldn't help myself. I shook hands with him.

"Charlie Reese," I said.

"Where you from?"

"Raleigh."

"Why're you here?"

He sure was nosy. But I figured if I laid out the cold hard truth, that would shut him up, and maybe he wouldn't want to be my Backpack Buddy anymore.

"My daddy's in jail and my mama won't get out of bed," I said.

Well, that boy didn't even blink an eye. "What's he in jail for?"

"Fighting."

"Why?"

"What do you mean?"

He wiped at his fogged-up glasses with the bottom of his T-shirt. His face was flushed pink in the damp heat of the bus. "Why was he fighting?" he said.

I shrugged. There was no telling why Scrappy was fighting. Besides, there were probably a bunch of other reasons he was in jail, but nobody ever tells me anything.

"Gus and Bertha told my mama you were coming. They go to my church and I gave them a cat one time," Howard said. "A scrawny gray cat that was living up under my porch."

Then he went on and on about how Gus taught him how to make a slingshot and how sometimes Bertha sells bread-and-butter pickles by the side of the road in the summer. How his mama drove her car right into the ditch beside Gus and Bertha's driveway one time and Gus pulled it out with a tractor and then they all ate barbecue sandwiches in the front yard.

"You'll like living with them," he said.

"I'm not *living* with them," I told him. "I'm going back to Raleigh."

"Oh." He looked down at his freckly hands in his lap. "When?"

"When my mama gets her feet on the ground."

"How long does that take?"

I shrugged. "Not long."

But the knot in my stomach told me that was a lie. The worry clutching at my heart told me my mama might never get her feet on the ground.

As the bus pulled out of the parking lot and headed toward town, Howard rattled off a list of school bus rules. No saving seats. No gum. No writing on the back of the seats. No cussing. A whole mess of rules that I was pretty sure nobody paid any mind to except maybe Howard.

11

I looked out the window at the sorry sights of Colby. A gas station. A trailer park. A laundromat. Wasn't much of a town, if you asked me. No malls or movie theaters. Not even a Chinese restaurant.

Before long, the bus was making its way up the mountain. The rain had stopped and wavy plumes of steam drifted up off the asphalt. The narrow road curved back and forth and round and round. Every now and then, the bus stopped to let some kid off at a pitiful-looking house with a red-dirt yard. We were almost to Gus and Bertha's when the bus stopped and Howard said, "See ya."

Another, younger-looking redheaded boy got off with him. I watched them make their way across the weed-filled yard to their house. Bikes and skateboards and footballs and sneakers were scattered from the front door to the road. A garden hose snaked from a dripping faucet to a hole in the yard. A small, dirty-faced boy was dropping rocks into the hole, sending up splashes of muddy water.

Howard waved as the bus pulled away, but I turned my eyes back to that dried-up gum.

When we finally got to Gus and Bertha's long gravel driveway, I got off and watched the bus drive away, making the rain-soaked Queen Anne's lace bob at the edge of the road. I was starting up the driveway when I noticed something shiny in the dirt at the edge of the road.

A penny!

I darted over and picked it up. Then I hurled it as far as I could and made my wish quick before that penny hit the road and bounced into the woods.

There! I'd gotten in my wish for the day.

Maybe this time it would finally come true.

Two

I trudged up the long driveway, jumping over puddles of muddy rainwater and wondering what Jackie was doing right that very minute. Probably smoking cigarettes with some boy in the parking lot of the Piggly Wiggly across from the high school. Everybody thinks my sister is an angel straight down from heaven, but I know better.

When Gus and Bertha's house finally came into view, I stopped. I'd been there four days already but I still couldn't get over how that house hung off the side of the mountain like it did. The front of the house sat smack on the ground with flowering shrubs nestled right up against it. But the back was on stilts stuck into the steep mountainside. On top of the stilts was a tiny porch with two rocking chairs and window boxes full of flowers perched on the railing.

On my first night in Colby, Gus had dragged a kitchen chair out there for me after supper. Bertha had asked me about a million questions, like what was my favorite subject in school and did I have a lucky number? Did I want to go swimming at the Y sometime and did I like boiled peanuts? But I just mumbled and shrugged till she finally stopped. I was too mad to talk. What was I doing there on that porch with these people I didn't even know? I felt like I'd been tossed out on the side of the road like a sack of unwanted kittens. So the three of us sat in silence, watching the sun sink behind the mountain and the lightning bugs twinkle off and on among the pine trees.

I'd spent the next three days trying to convince Gus and Bertha that it was dumb for me to go to school since it was almost summer. But the next thing I knew, I was sitting on that bus full of hillbilly kids on my way to school.

"Hey, there," Bertha called from the front door as I made my way across the yard. A fat orange cat darted out from behind the garden shed and trotted along beside me. Gus and Bertha had a whole passel of cats, sleeping under the porch, sunning on the windowsills, swatting bees out in the garden.

I went inside and dropped my backpack on Gus's

tattered easy chair. The smell of warm cinnamon drifted through the kitchen door.

"I made coffee cake," Bertha said. "I wonder why they call it coffee cake. Not a drop of coffee in it." She held the door open for the cat to come in. "Oh, I know. I bet 'cause you're supposed to drink coffee when you eat it. You think? Well, anyways, who cares, right?"

It had been clear to me from day one that Bertha was a talker. Not like her sister, my mama, who went for days without saying a word. I had been surprised when I saw how much they looked alike, though. Same mousy brown hair. Same long, thin fingers. Even the same crinkly lines along the sides of their mouths.

I sat at the kitchen table and watched Bertha cut a thick slice of coffee cake and put it on a paper towel in front of me. Then she pulled her chair close to mine and said, "Tell me every little thing about your first day. Your teacher. The other kids. What your classroom looks like. What you had for lunch. What you did at recess. Every little thing."

"Some girl ate a squirrel sandwich," I said.

Bertha's eyebrows shot up. "A squirrel sandwich? Are you sure?"

I licked my finger and pressed it on the paper towel

to get coffee cake crumbs. I nodded but I didn't look at her when I said, "I'm sure."

A small gray cat sat on the kitchen counter grooming himself. I wondered if that was the one Howard had given them. Bertha picked him up and kissed the top of his head. "Charlie don't want cat hair in her coffee cake, Walter." Then she gently put him down on the linoleum floor. His tail twitched as he watched a line of tiny ants marching from under the sink to a dark spot of something sticky by the stove.

"And there's an up-down boy in my class," I said.

Bertha cocked her head. "What in the name of sweet Bessie McGee is an up-down boy?" She snapped a brown leaf off of a plant on the windowsill and tucked it into her pocket.

"This boy named Howard who walks up and down, like this." I walked like Howard around the kitchen table.

"Howard Odom," Bertha said. "Bless his heart. Good as gold, that boy is. Don't bat an eye when kids poke fun at him, calling him names like Pogo." She shook her head. "I swear, kids can be so mean sometimes."

"Pogo?"

"Yeah, you know, like a pogo stick."

"He oughta punch their lights out," I said. "That's what I'd do."

Bertha widened her eyes at me, then shook her head. "Not that boy. He wouldn't hurt a fly. *All* them Odoms are like that. Good-hearted. Kinda wild sometimes, those brothers of his. But good-hearted." She brushed crumbs off the table and tossed them into the sink. "Shoot, just last week, three of those boys were over here helping Gus replace them boards on the porch that got eat up with termites and they wouldn't take one penny. We sent them home with a burlap bag full of turnips and they were happy as clams."

Turnips? Any kids who were happy about a bag of turnips must be weird, if you asked me.

Bertha sat at the table beside me again. "So what else?" she said. "Tell me something else about school."

I shrugged. I wasn't going to tell her about that "Getting to Know You" paper dropped onto Mrs. Willibey's desk like a hot potato or about Howard being my Backpack Buddy, so I just said, "Nothing."

"Nothing?"

"Nope."

Bertha slapped her hand on the kitchen table. "I almost forgot," she said. "I got you something." She motioned for me to follow her down the hall to the tiny spare room where I'd been sleeping.

"Ta-da!" She flung her arm out and grinned.

I followed her gaze to the narrow bed in the corner. Propped up against the wall were two pillows in pink pillowcases with Cinderella on them.

"I realized this morning that this room don't look one bit like a little girl's room," Bertha said. "So I went down to Big Lots and got those pillowcases. I was gonna get the matching bedspread but it was a double and not a twin. I might go back and get this fluffy pink rug they have if I can get Gus to help me move that bureau. And I know I need to get my canning jars out of here, and that old TV don't even work anymore but . . ."

She rambled on and on but I didn't even listen. *Cinderella pillowcases?* She must think I'm five instead of almost eleven. She sure didn't know much about kids.

That afternoon Jackie called from Raleigh. She told me how Carol Lee's cousin came to visit and gave her a cashmere sweater she didn't want anymore. And Carol Lee's daddy was teaching her how to drive since Scrappy never would. She said she was thinking about putting blue streaks in her hair and that some boy named Arlo was taking her to a NASCAR race down in Charlotte.

She was so busy telling me about her happy life that she didn't even ask me what it was like living in Colby with hillbilly kids who eat squirrel. After we hung up, I went back to my room and laid on the Cinderella pillows and felt sorry for myself. How could Jackie be so happy? It seemed like she didn't care one little bit about me anymore.

I bet Scrappy didn't care about me anymore, either. I bet he was so busy playing basketball behind the tall fence at the county jail that he didn't even think about me up here on this mountain in a house full of cats with these people I don't even know. And I knew for sure my mama wasn't thinking about me as she shuffled around the house in her bathrobe all red eyed and stoop shouldered.

I was definitely going to have to go out on that porch tonight and wait for the first star to come out so I could make my wish again. Maybe two in one day would do the trick.

Three

That night, out on the back porch with Gus and Bertha, I saw the first star, twinkling over the treetops. I closed my eyes and wished like crazy.

"Making a wish?" Gus asked.

I felt myself blush. "No."

Bertha nudged Gus. "Tell her about the time you wished your uncle Dean would disappear and then he did," she said.

Gus flapped his hand at her. "Aw, now, Bertie. She don't want to hear that boring ole story." He rocked his chair, making the porch floor creak and groan.

While Bertha talked a blue streak and hardly ever sat still, Gus was quiet and easygoing, with a calm, slow way about him. He wore a baseball cap all day and half the night, his scraggly brown hair poking out from under it every which way. The bill of his cap was dark brown with dirt and greasy fingerprints.

"That there is Pegasus," he said, pointing to a cluster of stars hovering way up over the top of the mountains in the distance.

"Gus should've been a scientist," Bertha said. "He can tell you everything you ever wanted to know about stars and air and plants and water and weather and all that stuff."

Gus let out a little *pfft*.

"He thinks I married him for his looks." Bertha winked at me. "But I married him for his brains," she said.

Gus laughed.

And then the most amazing thing happened. They both reached out at the exact same time and held hands. It was like somebody had said, "Okay, on the count of three, hold hands." I'd never in my whole life seen Scrappy and Mama hold hands. Shoot, most of the time, they didn't even look at each other.

I watched Gus and Bertha sitting there gazing at the night sky, the corners of their mouths turned up into contented smiles. Every now and then, Bertha looked dreamily over at Gus like he was a movie star and not some scraggly haired man who worked in a mattress factory over in Cooperville.

We stayed out there till it started to sprinkle again, a soft, cold rain that sent the cats at our feet darting inside.

I went to bed that night with my head swirling. I thought about Scrappy snoring away in the county jail and Mama staring up at the ceiling of her dark bedroom. I thought about Jackie, whispering gossip and painting her toenails with Carol Lee. I thought about Howard Odom with his up-down walk and his good-hearted family. And I thought about Gus and Bertha holding hands under the glow of Pegasus. And then I thought about my own pitiful self, laying there wondering if my wish would ever come true.

The next day, I wore Jackie's old white majorette boots to school. I knew I'd made a mistake the minute I got on the bus. As I made my way down the aisle, some of those girls pointed at my boots, giggling and whispering. I felt my face burn and I glared at them. Howard motioned for me to sit next to him, but I flopped down in the seat behind him.

I spent the morning drawing on my arm with a blue marker and pretending to read. At recess, Howard tried and tried to get me to let him show me around the school.

"I'm your Backpack Buddy, remember?" he said.

I shook my head. "Forget it," I said. "I'm not really interested. Besides, I'm not going to be here much longer."

"Why not?"

I rolled my eyes. "I *told* you. I'm going back to Raleigh."

"But what if your mama don't get her feet on the ground?" he said.

Well, what the heck kind of question was that? I stomped away from him and plopped down under the cafeteria windows and glared at the kids playing soccer on the playground. Once or twice I glanced over at Howard. He was drawing circles in the dirt with his foot and looking all mopey.

When the bell rang, everybody scrambled to line up. A bunch of wild boys pushed and shoved their way in front of Howard and he didn't even say anything. As I headed toward the line, a girl from my class named Audrey Mitchell waltzed right up to me and said, "Nice boots." She smirked while her friends giggled behind her.

I felt Scrappy's temper working its way from the tip

24

of my toes to the top of my head. Hot as fire. Then I said, "Thanks. They're good for kicking," and I kicked her skinny shin. Hard.

The next few minutes were a blur of crying and hollering and tattling and then I found myself sitting in front of Mr. Mason, the principal. While he lectured about my inappropriate behavior, I studied the inky little stars and hearts I had drawn on my arm that morning.

Mr. Mason asked me if I knew that what I did was wrong and would I like it if somebody did that to me and a bunch of other questions I didn't even care about.

I said "Yessir" and "No, sir" but I kept my eyes on my inky arm and clunked the heels of those majorette boots against the legs of my chair.

I shrugged when he said he was going to have to call Bertha and tell her what I'd done. Then I went back to my class and said I was sorry to Audrey Mitchell even though I wasn't really, and that was how my second day of school in Colby went.

That afternoon on the bus, Howard ignored my laser thoughts again and made a beeline right for me. He dropped into the seat next to me.

"You should save me a seat, 'cause I think Backpack Buddies are supposed to sit together," he said.

"That's against the rules," I said.

"I'm pretty sure you can save a seat for a Backpack Buddy."

I rolled my eyes and looked out the window.

"Why'd you kick Audrey Mitchell?" Howard asked.

I told him how she had said "nice boots" with that smirk on her face. He shook his head and said, "Dang, Charlie, why you gotta get so mad about that? That ain't nothing."

I shot him a glare. Maybe it was nothing to him, but it was something to me. I almost told him about my fiery temper that I got from Scrappy but I didn't. Instead, I told him how I got sent home from kindergarten the very first day for poking some boy with a pencil.

"Eraser end or pointy end?" Howard asked.

"Pointy."

"Dang, Charlie."

I shrugged. "I know. But I was mad."

"About *what*?"

"He stuck his thumb right through my sandwich," I said.

Howard shook his head again, making his red hair flop down over his glasses. "Here's what you do from now on," he said. "Every time you feel yourself starting to get mad, say 'Pineapple.'"

"Pineapple?"

"Yeah."

"Why?"

"That'll be like a code word to remind yourself to simmer down. Mama taught my little brother Cotton to say 'rutabaga' every time he gets the urge to draw on the wall."

"Does it work?"

"Sometimes."

That sounded like the dumbest thing I'd ever heard but I didn't say so. We sat in silence as the bus made its way up the narrow mountain road. Every once in a while, the view out the window changed from woods, thick with pine trees and ferns and moss-covered rocks, to a wide-open view of the mountains stretching on forever in the distance. A smoky haze hovered over them, soft gray against the deep blue of the mountains.

"That's why they're called the Blue Ridge Mountains," Gus had told me the first day I got to Colby. " 'Cause they're blue." Then he had gone on to explain how the color was because of something the pine trees released into the air. I didn't know what the heck he was talking about, but I had nodded like I did.

When the bus got to Howard's house, he grabbed his backpack and said, "Remember. Pineapple."

I watched him and his brother go up the rickety steps of their front porch and disappear inside the house, letting the screen door slam with a bang behind them. Next to the front door was a ratty-looking couch covered with a bedspread. Wilted yellowing plants and dried-up flowers planted in coffee cans lined the edges of the porch. Maybe the Odoms' hearts were so good that they didn't care that they lived in such a sad-looking house.

The bus chugged and groaned up the winding road. I was thinking about what I was going to say to Bertha about my kicking incident when a commotion outside the window caught my eye.

Two dogs were fighting in a dirt driveway beside a cluster of trailers. One was small and black. The other one was brown and black and skinny as all get-out. A little girl was screaming and carrying on while an old man turned on a garden hose and aimed a hard spray of water at the skinny dog.

"Get outta here!" he hollered.

A woman ran out of one of the trailers and tried to grab the black dog while the skinny dog snapped and growled and then suddenly just took off running. He ran along the edge of the road beside the bus for a minute or two, his long ears flapping in the breeze. I pressed my face against the window and watched him lope along the side of the road and then turn and disappear into the woods.

When I got off at Gus and Bertha's a few minutes later, I looked down at those majorette boots. Jackie had always looked so pretty in them but I looked dumb. Those girls were right to laugh at me.

That familiar mad feeling was settling over me like a blanket. But this time I was feeling mad at myself for being a loser that nobody wanted. I stomped my foot and then I kicked at gravel, sending it tumbling into the rhododendron bushes along the side of the driveway.

Then I whispered "Pineapple" before heading on up to Gus and Bertha's.

Four

I figured Bertha was gonna be mad at me for kicking that girl, but she surprised me by putting her arm around me and saying, "Tomorrow's a new day." Then she gave me a little squeeze and added, "Personally, I love those boots."

She didn't say one word about my inappropriate behavior. Mama would've hollered at me and reminded me for the umpteenth time that I was a troublemaker like Scrappy.

After supper that day, we had blueberry pie for dessert and I got to make my wish. If you cut off the pointed end of a slice of pie and save it for last, you can make a wish when you eat it. I had learned that from my cousin Melvin, who swore it had worked for him when his brother ran off and got married and left him with the bedroom all to himself.

I knew Gus and Bertha were watching me cut off that pointed piece and push it to the edge of my plate, but they didn't say anything. Even Bertha had been kind of quiet during supper. Maybe she really was mad at me for kicking Audrey. Maybe she was thinking, *The apple don't fall far from the tree.* Maybe that night in bed, she and Gus would whisper to each other how much I am like Scrappy and what in the world had they gotten themselves into when they agreed to let me stay with them.

After I ate that little pointed piece of pie and made my wish, I went out front to watch Gus do some weeding in the vegetable garden. A fluffy black cat rubbed against my legs, purring up a storm. I wrote my name in the dirt with a stick and then scribbled it out. There wasn't one blade of grass in that yard, just dirt and rocks, with sprinkles of color here and there. Patches of wildflowers nestled around the clothesline posts. The pink blooms of a dogwood tree over by the driveway. A neat row of daffodils lined up like soldiers along the edge of the chicken-wire fence that surrounded the garden.

Gus whistled while he hoed around the tiny tomato plants, stepping carefully between the pole beans and zucchini that were just beginning to poke through the warm spring dirt. On my very first day in Colby, Bertha had said to Gus, "Let's take Charlie on a tour of the garden!" So I had followed along behind them while they pointed out each little plant, telling me how the pole beans were gonna climb up the twine and the zucchini would have giant yellow flowers. I had nodded and said, "Oh," 'cause what else can you say about vegetables in a garden? But Gus? You would've thought that was the Garden of Eden out there the way he took care of it, examining each new leaf on the okra plants or moving a squash vine off of the walking path.

So while I scribbled in the red dirt, Gus whistled and hoed. Every now and then, he tugged on the bill of his cap or swatted at mosquitoes. I could hear Bertha in the kitchen talking to some of the cats while she fed them, scolding one of them for killing a bird. Telling another he was getting too fat.

I was about to go on back inside when something caught my eye. There was movement behind the tangle of shrubs that separated the yard from the woods. The black cat darted off, disappearing behind the shed over by the garden. I stood real still and squinted into the darkness of the woods. All of a sudden, a dog poked its head out from behind the bushes. A skinny brown-and-black dog with long, floppy ears. The same dog I'd seen fighting that afternoon!

He looked at me and cocked his head. I took one slow, tiptoeing step toward him. He ducked his head back a little, watching me. I took another step, and quick as lightning, he ran off into the woods.

"Dang it," I said.

"You say something?" Gus called from the garden.

"There was a dog over there." I pointed to the bushes.

"Brown and black? Floppy ears?"

"Yeah," I said. "Did you see him?"

"No, but I've seen him plenty of times before."

"Who does he belong to?"

Gus propped the hoe against the fence and sat in a lawn chair in the yard. "Just an ole wild stray," he said. "Been hanging around here for months. Bertha keeps putting table scraps out for him. He don't mind eating her meat loaf, but he don't want nothing else to do with her."

I looked toward the woods. "I bet I can catch him," I said.

Gus took off his baseball cap and scratched his head. "That ole mutt is mighty skittish."

"If I can catch him, can I keep him?"

"I think that dog would rather be a stray," he said.

But I knew better. I knew what it felt like to be a stray, not having a home where somebody wanted you. And he was a fighter. Like me. That dog and I had a lot in common. I was suddenly overwhelmed with love for that skinny dog.

I made a solemn vow and promise to myself right then and there. That dog was going to be mine.

Five

I thought I was glad when the weekend came 'cause I didn't have to go to school, but then Bertha told me we were going to church on Sunday.

I hadn't been to church since I was little. Scrappy never wanted any part of it, calling those people do-gooders and Bible-thumpers, but Mama took me and Jackie for a while. I didn't remember much about it except Jackie whining and complaining on the way there until Mama slapped her legs and told her to hush up. But then Mama got too nervous to drive and wouldn't take off her bathrobe or even comb her hair, so we stopped going.

When I walked into Bertha's kitchen on Sunday morning, she looked me up and down and said, "Oh, dear."

She wiped her hands on her apron. "Do you have a dress?"

I looked down at my jeans that were too short and my T-shirt that used to be Jackie's and shook my head.

Bertha flapped her hand at me. "Well, that's okay. We'll go shopping this week."

Then Gus came in the kitchen and I didn't hardly even recognize him. He had on a coat and tie! Instead of his usual muddy boots, he wore lace-up black shoes buffed and shiny. He could've passed for one of those fancy rich bankers over in Raleigh except for the garden dirt under his fingernails and his hair squashed flat from his baseball cap.

He sat at the kitchen table and Bertha kissed his cheek. "Well, look at you," she said, making him blush and swat her hand off of his shoulder. He kept pulling at his collar and wiping sweat off the back of his neck.

After breakfast, we headed down the mountain to Rocky Creek Baptist Church. When I got inside, I knew right away why Bertha had said "Oh, dear" when she saw me that morning. The other girls in church wore dresses. I couldn't look anybody in the eye, knowing my face was beet red and my jeans were all wrong.

I sat on the hard wooden pew, sandwiched between

Gus and Bertha. While the organist played church music, more and more people filed in, smiling and nodding at one another. Then Bertha poked me and whispered, "There's the Odoms."

I glanced up to see Howard and his family carrying their Bibles and making their way to the pew across the aisle. Five boys with slicked-down hair, poking each other and clomping too loud in their Sunday shoes. Their mama chatted with folks, asking about their sick grandmas and making on over their babies while their red-headed daddy mopped his face with a handkerchief.

After a prayer and a hymn, the kids had to go to their Sunday school classes. Imagine my surprise when I got to my class and there was Audrey Mitchell. She looked at me all wide-eyed, like I was a Martian right off of a spaceship. I sat as far away from her as I could, and then Howard came in with his up-down walk and sat next to me.

Our Sunday school teacher was a gray-haired, wrinkly-faced woman named Mrs. Mackey. She didn't waste one minute telling everybody that my name was Charlie Reese and please welcome me to their church family. Then she taught us a song called "Good Old Noah." Howard sang louder than anybody and, personally, I thought it was a little embarrassing, but nobody else seemed to pay him any mind.

After that, Mrs. Mackey told us we were going to play a game called Bible Detective. She would read questions from her Bible Detective cards and whenever you answered one right, you got a Bible buck. When you got enough Bible bucks, you could cash them in for a prize.

While she read the questions, the boys fidgeted and the girls whispered and giggled in their dresses, while I kept quiet in my ugly jeans.

How many braids were in Samson's hair?

Name the man who went down into a pit on a snowy day to kill a lion.

In what book, chapter, and verse can we read about a winner of a beauty contest becoming a queen?

Howard's hand shot up every time, but I knew for sure I was never going to win any Bible bucks.

After Sunday school, all the grownups and kids gathered in the fellowship hall. Bertha paraded me around like I was a beauty queen, introducing me to everybody and making on over me and saying how lucky she and Gus were to have me staying with them. People nodded and said, "Ain't that nice?" and stuff like that, but I bet they were wondering why my own mama and daddy couldn't take care of me and didn't I know girls don't wear jeans to church?

When Bertha introduced me to Howard's mama, she hugged me and said Howard had told her about me. Then she craned her neck, looking around the room. "Mr. Odom must be outside. And I'll never catch those wild boys of mine long enough to introduce you."

Some of the Odom boys chased each other around the room, their ties loose and their shirttails flapping. They grabbed brownies off of paper plates while Howard showed everybody his Bible bucks.

"But you come on by the house anytime, okay?" Mrs. Odom said.

Bertha grinned at me. "Now wouldn't that be nice, Charlie?"

I nodded and said, "Yes, ma'am," 'cause I knew that's what I was supposed to say.

When we finally climbed into the car and headed back up the mountain toward home, I scanned the woods and yards along the way, hoping I'd see that stray dog again, but I didn't. What I did see, though, was a truck full of hay. Jackie's friend Casey told me if you count to thirteen when you see a truck full of hay, you can make a wish. So, of course, that's exactly what I did.

. . .

Things at school seemed to get worse every day.

My homework papers came back all marked up by Mrs. Willibey in red pencil, with notes like "See me" and "Try again."

Sometimes I didn't even do my homework. It seemed like a waste of time since I wasn't going to be there much longer. Once in a while Bertha asked me if I had homework, and I was pretty good at just shrugging and changing the subject.

Besides, I was used to getting marked-up papers like that 'cause back in Raleigh, I wasn't exactly Student of the Year. Jackie was the only one who ever fussed at me for not going to school or not doing my homework, but I reminded her that she was not my mother so she should leave me alone. When my teacher called the house to tell Mama how bad I'd done on my math test or ask why I hadn't turned in my book report, Mama would holler and carry on for about five minutes and then she'd throw up her skinny arms and heave a big sigh before she said, "What's the use?" Then she'd shuffle out of the room in her bedroom slippers, muttering about how she didn't deserve that aggravation.

At least in Raleigh, I had friends at school, but here, when I sat at a table in the cafeteria, girls made faces like they smelled something bad and slid their trays away from me. Most days, I pretended like I had a stomachache and spent the afternoon in the nurse's office drawing more stars and hearts on my arm with a marker.

At recess, Howard followed me around, reminding me he was my Backpack Buddy and asking questions a mile a minute.

"Did you ever visit your daddy in jail?"

"Why ain't your sister here, too?"

"You want some of my Bible bucks?"

Sometimes I answered him and sometimes I didn't.

The thing about Howard was, everything just rolled right off him. It seemed like nothing bothered him one little bit. It was clear that nobody at school wanted much to do with him, but he didn't seem to mind. His brother Dwight was always surrounded by cussing, punching, ball-tossing, fist-bumping boys, but Howard never joined them. A couple of times when I rode into town with Gus and Bertha, I'd see his older brothers, Burl and Lenny, tossing a football or shooting hoops with their friends, but Howard would be sitting on the steps scribbling in a notebook or over by the garage fiddling with his bicycle.

Bertha had commented about him one day when we drove by. "That poor boy is too much of a loner," she said.

"Nothing wrong with that," Gus said.

Bertha shook her head. "Not for a child. Children need friends." Bertha sighed. "I don't get it. He's just as sweet as he can be."

"I bet it's 'cause of his up-down walk," I said.

"Well, that's mean," she said. She turned around to face me. "You're going to make so many new friends here in Colby, Charlie. I just know it."

I stared out the window and pretended like I wasn't even listening to her go on about all the things I could do. Like Girl Scouts and 4-H. She told me about her friend Jonelle who lived in Fairview and had a daughter my age. We could visit them some Saturday if I wanted to or maybe we could go to the mall down in Asheville. On and on she went, talking as if my life in Colby was going to be like living in Disney World.

"You're gonna talk that girl's head plum off, Bertie," Gus said.

Bertha laughed and slapped him playfully on the arm.

"Where do you think that dog is?" I asked Gus.

"Could be anywhere," he said. "That mutt gets around."

I'd been looking everywhere for that stray dog. I'd seen him twice since that day he'd come to Gus and Bertha's, but both times he darted off into the woods when he saw me.

"He sure loves my meat loaf, I can tell you that," Bertha said. "He licks that pan clean and then hightails it outta there so fast I hardly get so much as a glimpse of him."

I leaned back against the seat and sighed. I bet I was never gonna catch that dog. And what if I did? Could I really keep him? Mama would probably have a hissy fit. But I bet Scrappy would call from jail and tell her to stop her yammering and let me have a dog if I wanted one.

Then, as we were turning onto the main road into town, I saw a black horse out in a field, eating grass and swishing its tail at flies. I shook my fist at it three times and made my wish. That was the rule for black-horse wishing. If you see a white horse, just make a wish. But for a black horse you have to shake your fist at it three times. I'd learned that one from Scrappy, which made me a little skeptical, but I did it anyway.

Shook my fist and made my wish.

Six

A few days later, Mrs. Willibey called Bertha about my bad attitude. That day in school, she had asked me if I had two-thirds of a piece of pie and I wanted to give half to my sister, then how much of the whole pie would that be? I told her I wouldn't give my sister any of my pie. Everybody had laughed except Mrs. Willibey. She had turned red and pressed her lips together and made her eyes into little slits when she looked at me.

When she called Bertha that afternoon, I was stretched out in Gus's easy chair watching TV. The fat orange cat named Flora was curled in my lap.

I heard Bertha say "She did?" and "Oh, dear." Then she lowered her voice and I could only make out bits and pieces drifting through the kitchen door.

". . . a rough time . . ."

". . . missing her family . . ."

". . . been hard on her . . ."

Then she hung up and I kept my eyes on the TV when she came in and sat on the couch.

"That was Mrs. Willibey," she said.

A fast-talking guy on TV was pouring chocolate syrup on the floor and mopping it up with a Miracle Mop.

"She told me you've been a little rude in school," Bertha said.

Now the man on TV was showing the set of knives that came free with the Miracle Mop.

Then Bertha started going on about how she knows how upset I must be about my family being all broken like it is. Well, she didn't use the word *broken*, but she might as well have. She said she knew how it must be scary to see Mama like she was. How I must be worried sick about Scrappy. How I must miss Jackie so much.

I kept my eyes on the mopping man and in my head I said, *Pineapple. Pineapple. Pineapple.* But Howard's stupid idea didn't work because the next thing I knew I was hollering at Bertha. Mean words about minding her own business and who cared about my broken-up, sorry excuse for a family. Not me, that was for sure. The words kept spewing and got louder and faster. How I hated Colby and all those hillbilly kids and this nasty old house hanging off the side of the mountain and those canning jars in my room and especially those Cinderella pillowcases.

Then I stalked outside, letting the screen door slam behind me and trying not to think about Bertha sitting there on the couch looking like she'd been stabbed in the heart.

A couple of cats leaped out of my way as I stormed across the yard and up the driveway toward the road. I kicked at dirt and yanked on leaves and hurled gravel into the woods. When I got to the road, I didn't even care that the asphalt was burning hot under my bare feet. The mad was swirling inside me, making my ears ring and my stomach churn. But then, the next thing I knew, I was sitting in the dirt on the side of the road crying so hard I couldn't hardly breathe.

What was wrong with me? Why had I said those mean things to Bertha? Why was I acting so hateful at school? And then, while I was sitting there wallowing in my pity, somebody said, "What's the matter, Charlie?"

I looked up to see Howard standing by his bicycle in front of me.

I put my head on my knees and mumbled, "Nothing."

"Must be something," he said.

"Go away."

"Naw." He laid his bicycle in the weeds by the road and sat next to me. "You have to tell me what's the matter."

This boy beat all. He sure had a lot of gumption for a little ole redheaded up-down boy.

"I don't have to tell you anything," I said.

"Then you have to tell *somebody*." He pushed at his glasses.

"Why?"

"My mama says you should never keep your troubles to yourself. She says if you share 'em with somebody, they get smaller."

"Go away," I said.

"Did you kick somebody again?"

I shook my head.

"Poke 'em with a pencil?"

"No!" I hollered.

"Mama made this needlepoint sign that says, 'If all our troubles were hung on a line, you'd choose yours and I'd choose mine.'"

I lifted my head and stared at him. "What's that supposed to mean?" I asked him.

"It means everybody's got troubles and some of 'em

are worse than yours." He yanked at a blade of grass and tossed it into the road. "Or something like that," he added.

Ha! That was a good one. I couldn't think of anybody with worse troubles than me. Then I looked at Howard with his eyebrows knitted together and a look of pure worry on his face and before I knew it, I was spilling those troubles out to him. I told him how I wished Scrappy wasn't in jail. How he and I used to play poker and watch *Wheel of Fortune* and eat macaroni and cheese for breakfast. I told him how scared I was when I saw my mama crying into her pillow in her dark bedroom, not even caring one little bit whether I had clean clothes or even went to school. I told him how Mama and Scrappy would holler at each other the livelong day while me and Jackie sat on her bed with the radio turned up loud so we didn't have to hear them. I told him about all those times I watched from the bedroom window when Scrappy drove off with his tires screeching and gravel flying while Mama yelled "Good riddance to bad rubbish" from the front porch. I told him how much I missed Jackie, who knew all the words to nearly every song on the radio and would french braid my hair and share her nail polish with me. And then I told him those mean things I'd said to Bertha.

When I was done, the silence settled over us, still and soft, like a veil. The sun had gotten lower in the sky, sitting on top of the mountains in the distance, and the air had grown cooler.

For a minute, I thought maybe Howard was embarrassed by all that stuff I'd told him and didn't know what to say. I was starting to wish I had never shared my troubles with him like that. But then he looked right at me and said, "Want my advice?"

"Um, sure, I guess," I said.

"You can't do nothing about Scrappy and them back in Raleigh," he said. "The only thing you can fix is what you done to Bertha."

I guess he was right. I couldn't fix my mess of a family, but I could try to make things right with Bertha. I stood up and brushed the dirt off the back of my shorts. And then I couldn't hardly believe my eyes. Right there at the edge of the woods was that brown-and-black, floppy-eared dog!

I put my finger to my lips and went, "Shhhh."

The dog was watching me with his head cocked to the side.

"Don't move," I whispered to Howard.

I took one slow step toward the dog and guess what?

He wagged his tail! Two tiny little wags. That dog liked me.

"Hey, fella," I said, taking another step.

Then, wouldn't you know it, a car came roaring up the road and whizzed past us and that dog darted off into the woods.

I stamped my foot. "Dang it!"

I'd almost forgotten Howard was there when he said, "I've seen that dog before."

"He's mine," I said.

"Really?"

"Well, he's gonna be."

"I bet he's full of ticks," he said. "And he might have the mange. Stray dogs have the mange."

"So what?" I said. "His name is Wishbone." The minute I said that, it felt right. Wishbone. That was the perfect name for my dog.

"I'm going to catch him," I said. "Then I'll bathe him and get the ticks off him and teach him tricks and let him sleep in the bed with me."

"I'll help you catch him," Howard said, picking his bike up out of the weeds.

"You will?"

"Sure."

Suddenly Howard seemed different. He didn't seem so much like a nosy up-down boy, nagging me half to death about being my Backpack Buddy. He seemed more like somebody being nice to me. Somebody I had shared my troubles with.

I watched him get on his bike and pedal off toward his house. Then I called "Bye, Wishbone" into the woods before I hurried up the road to make things right with Bertha.

Seven

By the time I got home, it was getting dark. Gus's old rattletrap of a car was in the driveway and the smell of spaghetti sauce drifted through the screen door.

My feet felt like cinder blocks as I made my way across the yard toward the house. More than anything, I wanted to just go on back to my room and pretend like this day had never happened.

But I didn't.

I put one cinder-block foot in front of the other until I was on the back porch, where Gus and Bertha sat gazing out at the mountain view.

"Hey," I said, and my voice sounded like a sniveling baby. I kept my eyes on the leaf-covered floorboards of the porch.

"Hey, there," Gus said.

I couldn't look at Bertha, but her silence smacked me hard. I sat down and studied the fading hearts and stars I'd drawn on my arm. From somewhere way down in the woods, a bullfrog croaked, sending his deep-throated call echoing out into the cool evening air.

I counted to three in my head and then I said it. "I'm sorry, Bertha."

Then I did what I'd told myself I most definitely would not do.

I cried.

And, I swear, I could not stop no matter how much I wanted to.

The worst part was that I couldn't get myself to tell Bertha those things I'd practiced in my head. Like how I didn't mean to holler at her. How I don't hate this house perched on the mountainside with Pegasus up there shining over the porch. How those canning jars don't bother me one little bit. And most of all, how I love Cinderella, because who doesn't?

But all I did was cry. And then Bertha was kneeling in front of me with her warm hand on my ink-stained arm.

"You are a blessing in this house, Charlie," she said.

A blessing?

She should've called me mean and hateful and dumb and sorry, but she called me a blessing.

Then Gus stood up and said the perfect Gus thing.

"Let's have some of that blackberry cobbler before supper."

So that's what we did.

The three of us sat out on the porch as the stars were beginning to twinkle up in the Carolina sky and ate blackberry cobbler before supper. And while Bertha told us about how her friend Racine backed her car into the flagpole at the post office that afternoon and then just drove on off like nothing had even happened, an acorn dropped from the branches of the oak tree hanging over the porch and fell right at my feet.

I nearly spilled my cobbler when I jumped up and grabbed it. I had almost let that day slip by without making my wish, and now here came an acorn like it was dropped right down from heaven. I hesitated, but then I went on and did what I had to do. I turned in a circle three times, clutching that acorn tight and making my wish.

Then I went back to my room and set the acorn on the windowsill. I would leave it there for three days to make sure my wish would be even stronger. That's what my Girl Scout leader in Raleigh told me about acorn wishes, and that could not be a lie because Girl Scout leaders do not lie.

After supper, we had more blackberry cobbler. Gus went out to the garden to make sure the sprinkler was turned off, and Bertha said, "Stay right here, Charlie. I want to show you something."

She went to her room and came back with a tattered shoebox. She took the lid off and said, "Look."

I peered inside. Photographs.

Bertha rummaged through them and took one out. She smiled at it and handed it to me.

"Your mama and me," she said, pointing to the hand-writing on the back. *Bertha and Carla*, in big printed letters.

I took the faded photograph from her.

Two young girls sat on the hood of a car with their arms around each other.

"Which one's Mama?" I asked.

Bertha pointed to the smaller girl. I squinted down at her. She was missing her two front teeth and had a Band-Aid on her elbow.

I could not take my eyes off of that girl. I imagined her getting down from that car and skipping in circles.

I imagined her singing with her big sister, Bertha, in the backseat of their daddy's car. I imagined her telling knock-knock jokes and roller-skating and eating ice cream on her porch at night.

When had this gap-toothed little girl turned into that sad woman in her dark bedroom in Raleigh?

"Did y'all love each other?" I asked Bertha.

"We sure did." Then she showed me some more photographs. Mama opening a present beside a Christmas tree. The two of them playing with a puppy in the snow. Bertha pulling Mama in a wagon on a dirt road.

"Why don't y'all see each other anymore?" I said.

Bertha let out a big sigh and shook her head. "We grew up," she said. "When you grow up, sometimes life gets complicated."

That wasn't a very good answer, but I could tell it was the only one I was going to get, so I just said, "Oh."

When Gus came back in from the garden, we went out on the porch. They held hands while Bertha told us about some old man selling moldy strawberries from the back of a truck out on Highway 14. Then she said, "You can call Jackie tomorrow if you want to, Charlie."

"No, thanks," I said.

It was so quiet I could hear Bertha breathing. I could feel her looking at me but I stared out at the treetops.

"Charlie," she said. "Don't be mad at Jackie."

"I'm not mad at Jackie," I said, but that lie was like a dark cloud settling over us.

I *was* mad at Jackie. She acted like she didn't have one single trouble hanging on her line and she didn't care one bit about me.

Then we sat there in silence, breathing in the cool night air and listening to the crickets under the porch.

That night when I went to bed, I laid there in the dark and pictured a clothesline full of somebody else's troubles. I knew for sure there were a lot of them I'd rather pluck off of that line than mine. I imagined what the other troubles might be. There would probably be toothaches and failed math tests. Lost cats and ugly hair. Cheating boyfriends and broken-down cars. But none of those could hold a candle to my troubles, weighing down that clothesline like a sack full of bricks.

I tiptoed to the window and stared out into the night, thinking maybe I'd see a falling star to wish on. The moon was bright over the mountains and sent a shimmering glow across the yard, making shadows that snaked around the dogwood tree and crept along the garden fence.

I knew Wishbone was out there somewhere all by himself. I wondered what he was doing. Eating stale bread out of someone's garbage? Trotting along the highway in the moonlight? Sleeping under somebody's porch?

I hoped Gus wasn't right about Wishbone wanting to be a stray. But then I remembered how he had wagged his tail at me that day. He liked me. I was sure of it. And if he was mine and didn't have to be a stray anymore, I bet he would love me.

I clasped my hands together like I was praying and whispered into the darkness, "Please come back, Wishbone."

Eight

On Saturday, Howard was going to help me look for Wishbone, but first I had to go shopping with Bertha.

"I haven't been to Asheville in ages," she said, getting behind the wheel of Gus's old car. It started with a rumble, sending puffs of black smoke drifting out of the tailpipe and floating over the yard.

As we wound our way down the mountain and onto the highway, Bertha chattered nonstop. She told me about the time she and Gus went camping and a baby bear got into their cooler and stole their hot dogs.

"Can you believe that?" she said. "A bear eating hot dogs!"

She talked about how much she hated snakes, and how when a tiny brown garter snake got in the house once, she stayed with her friend Jonelle for nearly a week until Gus swore on the Bible that it was gone.

And she could hardly stop laughing long enough to tell me about the time some guy named Arthur Kruger got drunk and lost his false teeth at the church picnic.

"I didn't even want to think about where those teeth would turn up," she said, wiping her eyes. "I didn't eat any more potato salad after that, that's for sure."

Finally I figured I'd have to interrupt her, so I did.

"But what about you and Mama?" I asked.

"What do you mean?"

"Tell me something about y'all."

"Oh, well, um, let's see now . . ."

I waited, watching her face. Seeing her searching for just the right thing to tell me.

"When I was about ten," she said, "so, let's see, Carla would've been about seven, we spent the whole summer making yarn bracelets to sell so we could buy fish for an aquarium our uncle gave us."

Yarn bracelets?

I wondered how come Mama never showed me how to make yarn bracelets.

"Then," Bertha went on, "this mean boy who lived across the street from us threw every one of those bracelets up into the hickory nut tree in our front yard. Way up in the branches so we couldn't get them down." She shook her head. "Isn't that so mean?"

"What did y'all do?"

"Well, that's why I'm telling this story, 'cause it's just so like Carla," she said. "She stomped over to that boy and bit him on the hand so hard he hollered like she'd cut his hand off with a butcher knife. Then he ran home crying while she hollered cuss words at him."

Bertha chuckled. "That girl had some kinda temper," she said.

A temper?

Maybe I didn't get my temper from Scrappy, after all. Maybe I got my temper from Mama.

I hesitated, but then I decided to just go for it. "How come y'all stopped seeing each other?" I asked, hoping maybe this time she'd give me a better answer than she had before.

Bertha stared out at the road ahead. "Well, you know, when we got to be teenagers we were so busy with this, that, and the other thing. And then she dropped out of high school and the next thing I knew she was hightailing it to Raleigh."

"But how come y'all never see each other now?"

Bertha pressed her lips together and shot me a look out of the corner of her eye. "It's kind of complicated, Charlie," she said.

There it was again. Another not-very-good answer.

So we drove on in silence until we got to Asheville. At the mall, I couldn't help but think about Jackie. She and I used to spend all day at the mall, wandering from store to store trying on crop tops and miniskirts that we were never allowed to have. Picking out earrings we would buy if our ears were pierced. Spritzing fancy perfume on each other from the samples at the cosmetics counter.

"Let's go to Sears and look for Sunday school dresses," Bertha said.

So we shopped all morning, and by the time we headed back to Colby, I had two new dresses and a lavender cardigan sweater. Bertha thought one of the dresses might be too short for church but she bought it anyway.

When we got home, Howard was sitting in a lawn chair by the garden watching Gus doing some repairs to the fence.

"Hey, there!" Bertha called.

Howard walked his up-down walk over to the car as I was getting my shopping bags out of the backseat.

"Hey," he said to Bertha. Then he turned to me and said, "I drew a map."

62

"What for?"

"To help us look for Wishbone." He took a piece of folded-up notebook paper out of his pocket to show me. "I figured we could mark the places we look and it will help us keep track."

I shrugged. "Okay."

Bertha reached for the shopping bags. "I'll take those inside," she said.

Then me and Howard headed off toward the road, peering into tangled shrubs and squinting into the dark woods along the way. Howard thought we should check the path where we had seen him yesterday.

"I bet he hangs out there a lot," he said.

"Maybe." I pushed some tall weeds aside and jumped over the shallow ditch that ran along the edge of the road. "But Gus said he's liable to be anywhere," I added.

We looked and looked, climbing over fallen trees and pushing through prickly vines. But after a while, we were hot and tired and hadn't seen a single sign of Wishbone. So Howard whipped out his map and a stubby pencil and marked the places we had looked, and we decided to call it a day.

The next day, I marched into Sunday school in my new dress and plopped right down next to Audrey. I said, "Hey," but she acted like I was invisible. I guess she forgot I was part of her church family.

First, we had to play that Bible Detective game again, and Howard added to his collection of Bible bucks. I couldn't get over all the stuff he knew about the Bible.

What was Moses's brother's name?

How many times a day did ravens bring food to Elijah?

Audrey waved her hand almost as much as Howard did, jangling her bracelets and going, "I know! I know!"

After that, Mrs. Mackey told us we were going to decorate the bulletin board in the fellowship hall and it would be called *Our Garden of Blessings.*

"We'll be making a garden of flowers to show our many blessings," she said. Then she explained that we would make construction paper flowers and write one of our many blessings on each one.

I confess I wasn't too clear exactly what that meant, but I followed everybody else and got colored paper and glue and scissors. I worked real slow, hoping I could see what somebody else was doing. Sure enough, Audrey finished her first flower, a big yellow daisy. Then she used a blue crayon to write on one of the petals: "My family."

My stomach squeezed up and my face felt hot. I put my hands in my lap so nobody could see them shaking.

That yellow daisy laid there on the table in front of me reminding me that I did not belong here. Letting me know that even though I was here in church in my new dress, I did not have a blessing.

"May I be excused?" I said to Mrs. Mackey. But I didn't even wait for her to answer. I hurried out of that room and went outside to the parking lot.

But before I had time to start feeling sorry for myself, something good happened. I saw a red bird. A big, bright cardinal on the telephone line across the street. I closed my eyes, spit three times, and made my wish.

Nine

"Come to my house after school tomorrow," Howard said on the bus the next morning. "I have a plan."

"What kind of plan?" I asked.

"A plan for catching that dog."

"Wishbone," I said. "His name is Wishbone."

Howard took a bite of the toast he had brought on the bus with him. "Whatever," he said. "We still need a better plan than a map."

"I don't see why we can't—" I sat up and grabbed Howard's knee. "Don't move," I said.

His eyes got wide. "What's wrong?"

"Take off your glasses," I said. "Real slow."

"Why?"

"Just do it," I snapped, a little louder than I'd meant to.

He took his glasses off and then squinted over at me.

"There's an eyelash right there," I said, pointing to one of the thick lenses. "I need it."

"Why?"

"To make a wish."

"A wish?"

"If you blow on an eyelash, you get to make a wish." I took the glasses from him and pressed my finger on the lens. Then I held it up so Howard could see the tiny, reddish eyelash. "See?" I said.

Then I closed my eyes, made my wish, and blew, sending that eyelash out into the air where it disappeared, probably settling on the floor with clumps of dirt and chewed gum and trampled spelling tests.

"What'd you wish for?" Howard asked.

"I can't tell you," I said.

"Why not?"

I flopped back against the seat and rolled my eyes. "Jeez, Howard," I said.

"What?"

I explained to him that if you tell your wish, then it won't come true. "Everybody knows that," I added.

Howard wiped his glasses with the end of his T-shirt and put them back on.

"I've made a wish every single day since fourth grade," I said.

Howard bugged his eyes out at me. "You must want a lot of stuff."

I shook my head. "No, just one thing," I said. "I always wish for the same thing. Every single time."

The minute I said that, I regretted it. I knew what he was going to say next and sure enough, he did.

"Well, if you're making the same wish every time, it must not be coming true," he said. "So what's the point? Seems kind of dumb to me."

I felt my face turning red and that familiar feeling of anger starting to churn in my stomach. "Because some day it *will* come true!" I hollered, making a bunch of kids turn in their seats and stare at me.

Howard looked at me over the top of his glasses and said, "Pineapple."

I kicked his backpack hard, sending it sliding out into the aisle of the bus. I confess to feeling a flicker of regret when some kids laughed at that. But Howard, he just picked it up, brushed the dirt off of it, and said, "Pineapple, Charlie. Remember?"

I held on to my mad feelings all morning, taking every opportunity I could to shoot razor-sharp glares at Howard or to bump into him real hard over by the pencil sharpener. I never should've told him about my wishing. I'd never told anybody and now that I had, it *did* sound dumb. Why *would* anyone make the same wish every day if it never came true? Maybe I should give up.

But then guess what happened? I looked at the clock and it was 11:11! I closed my eyes and made my wish.

By the time I got home from school, my mad feelings about Howard were gone and I was glad he had a plan to catch Wishbone. When I told Bertha I was going to his house the next day, she was tickled pink. She kept telling me how good I was to be friends with Howard 'cause other kids were so mean to him.

"Even in *church*," she said. "Can you believe that?"

I didn't tell her I sure could believe that, with the likes of Audrey Mitchell in that so-called church family.

That afternoon, Howard dropped into the seat next to me and said, "You can borrow my brother Lenny's bike."

"What for?"

"So you can get home. Better than walking." He took a smashed bag of potato chips out of his backpack and emptied the crumbs into his mouth. "I got a real good plan," he said. "You know. For catching Wishbone."

And wasn't that just like Howard, to go right on wanting to help me after I'd kicked his backpack and been mean to him like I had yesterday?

So when the bus stopped at his house, I followed him and Dwight across the weed-filled yard, up the rickety steps, past the ratty couch, and into that sad-looking house. When I stepped inside, I didn't know where to look first. A hamster cage on the coffee table. A drum set in the corner. Stacks of books and magazines lining the walls. Some kind of tree planted in a rusty bucket by the window. The floor was littered with blankets and pillows and shoes and board games and plastic bowls with popcorn kernels and pretzel crumbs in the bottom.

The walls were covered with crayon artwork on construction paper and school papers with gold star stickers and "Nice job!" written at the top. I could see that Mrs. Odom's rutabaga trick with Howard's brother Cotton wasn't working too good because there were lots of drawings with colored markers along the bottom of the walls.

Howard stepped over the pillows and stuff and motioned for me to follow him into the kitchen.

"Mama," he said, "Charlie's here."

Mrs. Odom turned from the sink and smiled the nicest smile. "Well, hey!" She wiped her hands on her apron and put her arm around my shoulder and gave me a little squeeze. "Howard told me you're his Backpack Buddy at school," she said. "And about that Wishbone dog." Then she started going on about how Gus and Bertha were so happy to have me here in Colby with them and weren't the Blue Ridge Mountains heaven on earth? After that she put a cake with pink and purple flowers in a cardboard box from the grocery store on the kitchen table and told us to have some. The next thing I knew, that little kitchen was filled with boys pushing and poking and grabbing at that cake. They didn't even use plates or forks or anything. Just cut a slice and ate it right there, dropping crumbs on the floor and Mrs. Odom didn't seem to mind one bit.

The oldest boy was Burl, the only dark-haired one. Loud-talking and friendly-faced, with a shadow of a mustache over his lip. Next was Lenny, in a grease-stained T-shirt. His freckled arms were long and skinny and he kept punching Dwight and elbowing Burl. Next came Howard and Dwight, who were only a year or two apart and could have passed for twins except Howard wore glasses and had that up-down walk. And the youngest was Cotton, dirty-faced and sticky-fingered. Legs all covered in scrapes and bruises and Band-Aids.

Mrs. Odom gave us water in paper cups and made the

rounds kissing and hugging each of those boys. It didn't take a genius to know that Bertha had been right about the Odoms and their good hearts. I don't know why, but I felt shy and out of place in there with the noise and energy bouncing around and sheer goodness clinging to the walls of that house.

Howard and I sat on the couch on the porch and he told me about his plan to catch Wishbone. He had it all written down in a notebook and even had pictures drawn with colored pencils.

"You think it'll work?" I asked.

"Sure." Howard closed his notebook and hugged it to his chest. Then we sat in silence watching Lenny and Cotton filling a plastic bucket with rocks and dragging it to the side of the yard where they were building some kind of wall.

Dwight rode his bike round and round the yard, stirring up clouds of red dust while Burl hollered at him to stop 'cause he was trying to change the oil in his truck.

Then me and Howard decided to look for Wishbone some more, so we spent the rest of the afternoon tromping through the woods and wandering up and down the side of the road but finally gave up. By the time we got back to Howard's house, Mrs. Odom was telling everybody to wash up for supper.

"Stay and have supper with us, Charlie," she said.

Before I could say anything, Mrs. Odom added, "I'll call Bertha and see if it's okay with her. Mr. Odom's driving a load of lumber over to Charlotte, so you can sit right there in his chair."

So we sat at the table and before I knew what was happening, Howard grabbed my right hand and Dwight grabbed my left and they all bowed their heads while Burl said the blessing. He thanked the Lord for nearly everything under the sun, including the deviled eggs on the plate in front of him.

Then everybody said "Amen" and dove into that food like they hadn't eaten in a week.

Mrs. Odom kept jumping up to get more pork chops or pour more milk, and it seemed like she couldn't walk by one of those boys without patting their shoulders or kissing the tops of their heads.

I tried to imagine taking Howard to my house back in Raleigh. So quiet and dark. My school papers would not be taped on the wall and Mama would not kiss me on the top of my head. There wouldn't be any cake with pink and purple flowers. If Howard stayed for supper, he and I would eat pork and beans or potato chips or a bologna sandwich in front of the TV and nobody would say the blessing.

When it was time for me to leave, I thanked Mrs. Odom, climbed on Lenny's bike, and set off for home. As I pedaled up the road, I turned and glanced back at the Odoms' house. I remembered that first day on the school bus when I had seen it and thought it was so sad-looking. Then I pictured all those boys in that little kitchen getting loved on by their mama and that house didn't look one bit sad anymore.

Ten

When I got home, I told Gus and Bertha about Howard's plan to catch Wishbone.

"We're gonna build a great big trap," I said, stretching my arms out to show how big. "With chicken wire from his daddy's workshop."

Gus's eyebrows shot up. "A trap, huh?"

I nodded. "Well, kind of. More like one of those big dog crates. We're gonna put it out at the edge of the woods beside the garden shed and then we're gonna stick branches and leaves and stuff in the chicken wire so it blends in."

I went on to explain how we were going to put something good to eat inside the crate and when Wishbone went in to eat it, we'd close the door.

"He likes meat loaf," Bertha said. "And hot dogs. And bologna." She tossed a couple of pieces of fish stick left over from supper onto the floor for two of the cats. "Now, I don't want to rain on your parade, Charlie, but what if that dog isn't friendly to people? What if he bites? What if he has some kind of dog disease?"

"He won't bite. He likes me," I said, ignoring that question about dog disease.

"Gus," Bertha said, "tell Charlie about that dog you had when you were a kid." And then she went and told me about Gus's dog named Skeeter who used to catch rabbits and bring them home for Gus and his sisters to play with. "And one time he climbed in the back of a produce truck and ended up all the way down in Hendersonville and showed up on the front porch the next day full of porcupine quills. Right, Gus?"

Gus nodded. "Right."

"And then one time he dug up a hornet's nest," Bertha said. "That dog must've had nine lives, like a cat."

"Must have," Gus said.

"Tell her about how he waited for you outside school every day." Bertha scooped one of the cats onto her lap. "Oh, and tell her about how he used to steal chicken livers right out of the frying pan."

"We're gonna bore this poor child to death, Bertie," he said, winking at me. "Right, Butterbean?"

Gus had started calling me Butterbean sometimes. That made me feel like a baby, but I didn't say anything.

Then Bertha told us about some woman in the grocery store who fainted in the cereal aisle but I wasn't really listening because I was thinking about Wishbone. I pictured him waiting at school for me every day. Then he'd run along beside the school bus like he'd done that day I saw him fighting. Maybe the bus driver would let him *on* the bus because he was so smart and would do tricks for all the kids.

He'd sleep in my bed every night and I'd sing "Good Old Noah" to him. He'd let me put Jackie's Raleigh High School T-shirt on him and maybe even paint his toenails red. I'd teach him to go up to the end of the driveway on Sunday mornings and get the newspaper before church. He'd chase rabbits out of the garden and sit out on the porch with us every night. I still had a little niggle about Mama having a hissy fit when I brought him back to Raleigh with me, but I pushed that aside.

By the time Bertha went inside to get a box of graham crackers for us, I was so in love with Wishbone I couldn't hardly stand it. I sure hoped Howard's plan worked.

"Let's go set up the sprinkler in the garden," Gus said to me, tugging on his dirty baseball cap.

I followed him outside, with three cats sauntering along behind us. I helped him untangle the hose and drag it out to the garden. While he attached the sprinkler to it, I walked up and down the tidy rows of pole beans and squash and tomato plants growing bigger every day. The soft dirt was warm under my bare feet. Suddenly, a ladybug landed on my arm! I put my finger next to it and let it climb on. Then I held my finger up and whispered, "Ladybug, ladybug, fly away home." As I watched that little ladybug fly off into the sky, I made my wish.

Jackie called again that night. She told me she had put those blue streaks in her hair and now everybody at school was copying her.

"I swear, Charlie," she said. "Everybody in Raleigh's got blue streaks in their hair."

Then she told me she met some boy who played guitar in a band and had his nose pierced. His name was Cockroach, and her sorta-kinda boyfriend, Arlo, didn't like him.

"Cockroach?" I said, because what else can you say to that?

But she just kept on talking. She couldn't wait to

graduate and kiss that school goodbye. She and some girl named Shayla might move to Fort Lauderdale if Shayla's uncle could get them jobs in his Mexican restaurant. But if that didn't happen, she might go to school to be a dental assistant.

She sure had a lot of plans but it seemed like none of them included me.

"Are you gonna come visit me sometime?" I asked in a tiny voice that sounded like a baby.

"Of course I am, Charlie," she said. "As soon as I get time."

I guess she had lots of time for Cockroach but not much time for me.

Out on the porch that night, Bertha told Gus about her day while I sent my thoughts zipping through the trees to wherever Wishbone was. I wanted him to know he didn't have to be a stray like me. I wanted him to be mine.

Then my mind wandered to the Odoms. I wondered what they were doing right that very minute. I bet they were all piled on pillows on the floor eating popcorn and playing Crazy Eights. I bet Mrs. Odom was taping their school papers up on the wall and telling them how proud she was of them. Then she'd have to say "rutabaga" so Cotton would stop drawing on the wall with markers.

Gus interrupted my thoughts when he stood up and stretched and said, "Time to turn in."

I hated the thought of another day at school. That awful bus with gum on the seats and kids snickering when I walked by. Mrs. Willibey frowning at me and tossing my marked-up papers onto my desk with a sigh. The cafeteria with kids flinging peas at each other and ignoring me. There were only a few more weeks of school left but it felt like a hundred years to me.

There was no doubt about it. I needed Wishbone more than ever.

Eleven

The next day at school, it seemed like the clock had stopped and the day was stuck in a never-ending torture of math and social studies and gym. Even lunch and recess were in slow motion. Finally the dismissal bell rang and I hightailed it to the bus. I plopped down in my usual spot and waited for Howard. He must've been taking his own sweet time because the seats were starting to fill up. The next thing I knew, Audrey Mitchell was making her way up the aisle, cutting her eyes from side to side searching for a seat. I couldn't believe it when she sat next to me, propping her backpack between us so she wouldn't catch any of my cooties.

"You can't sit here," I said.

She made an ugly face at me and said, "Yes, I can."

"No, you can't!" I sort of hollered.

She flinched a little and gaped at me. "You can't save seats," she said. "That's the rule."

Pineapple.

Pineapple.

Pineapple.

But Howard's dumb trick didn't work because the next thing I knew, I had shoved her right off the seat and into the aisle. The minute I did it, I regretted it. Everybody liked Audrey. I ought to be bringing her candy bars and telling her how nice her hair looked instead of shoving her onto the dirty bus floor. Luckily, Audrey didn't have a temper like me and Scrappy. All she did was yelp a little bit, dust herself off, call me crazy, and move to another seat.

By the time Howard finally got there, my temper had settled down from a boil to a simmer.

He dropped into the seat next to me. "What you fired up about now?" he asked.

I looked out the window so he couldn't see my still-red face.

"I'm not fired up," I said.

He pushed his glasses up on his nose and went, "Huh." Then he dug around in his backpack and pulled out half a cheese sandwich. He took the cheese out, rolled it into a ball and popped it into his mouth. Then he did the same with the bread, rolling it into doughy balls.

As the bus made its way through the streets of Colby, I thought about that trap we were gonna make to catch Wishbone, and my simmering anger disappeared. In its place was a swirl of excitement.

When we got to Howard's, Mrs. Odom was on the porch with Cotton, smiling and waving to the bus driver. Howard, Dwight, and me sat on the porch steps while she asked about our day. Did Mrs. Willibey finally get that window fan fixed? Was Dwight's math test hard? Did the PTA sell cupcakes in the cafeteria again?

Then Howard whipped some papers out of his backpack and thrust them at her, grinning. "Ta-da!" he said.

She made such a fuss over those papers you'd've thought they were made of pure gold. I could practically feel my marked-up papers jammed into the bottom of my backpack, weighing heavy on my lap. I wished I had a good one so I could say "ta-da" too.

Howard didn't really need to be my Backpack Buddy anymore since I knew my way around school and I definitely knew the rules. Instead, he kept offering to help me with some of my schoolwork. I always said no, 'cause what was the use? I wasn't even going to be at that school much longer, I reminded him. His face would droop and he'd say, "You never know. You might be."

I ignored that and stuffed my sorry-looking papers into my backpack like I didn't even care one bit. But sitting on that porch with Mrs. Odom, I sort of wished I had let him help me some.

After we had banana pudding for a snack, me and Howard went straight back to the ramshackle garage behind his house. I swear, that garage looked like it was going to fall right over, tilting sideways with the door hanging off one hinge. We stepped inside and Howard's daddy looked up from his workbench in the corner. When he stood up, I thought his head was going to go right through the ceiling, he was so tall. He had great big freckled hands and fiery red hair and twinkly blue eyes. He smelled like grass and sawdust and gasoline all mixed together.

"Hey, there," he said, and his big booming voice bounced around that little garage, practically shaking the saws and shovels right off the walls.

I'd seen him at church, mopping his sweaty face with a handkerchief while he belted out "When the Roll Is Called Up Yonder," but I'd never talked to him. While most folks were drinking coffee and chitchatting in the fellowship hall, Mr. Odom and some of the other men were outside inspecting each other's truck engines or watching teenagers play basketball in the parking lot.

"Well, look at you," he said to me. "You know, you are the spitting image of your mama."

My mama?

I hadn't expected *that*.

"I am?" I asked.

"You sure are. Look just like her."

"You mean Bertha?" I said.

"Naw, Carla," he said. "Your mama."

"You know her?"

"Don't really know her," he said. "Only seen her a time or two."

"In Raleigh, you mean?"

"Naw, up yonder at Gus and Bertha's." He brushed sawdust off the front of his shirt. "Seems like just yesterday, but I reckon it wasn't," he said.

"Oh," was all I could think of to say, but my mind was racing. When had Mama been at Gus and Bertha's? How come nobody'd ever told me that?

"Old Howie here has been talking about you nonstop," he said, winking at Howard.

I felt my cheeks burn.

Then Mr. Odom said, "So, y'all gonna catch that mangy old hound, are you?"

"Yessir."

"That mutt's a rascal. I can tell you that. Been chased away from every chicken coop and garbage can in Colby."

"His name is Wishbone," Howard said.

Mr. Odom chuckled. "Well, that's a fine name."

"He likes me," I said.

"Charlie's gonna keep him," Howard said. "But we have to catch him first."

So Mr. Odom showed us how to staple chicken wire to wood and how to screw on hinges for a door, and before long, we had a trap perfect for catching a dog. When Burl got home from his job pumping gas, he helped us load the trap into the back of his truck and drove us to Gus and Bertha's. My thoughts kept flitting around all over the place, sometimes thinking about Wishbone and sometimes thinking about Mama being up there at Gus and Bertha's. But Burl played the radio so loud none of my flitting thoughts had a chance to settle down in one place.

When we got to Gus and Bertha's, we set the trap up over by the bushes at the edge of the yard. While me and

Howard gathered leaves and branches to stick through the chicken wire, Bertha kept Burl busy with all her questions.

Did he think his mama would like some pickled okra from the garden when it was ready?

Was Lenny still in the marching band?

Had his grandmama had that hip surgery yet?

Burl said, "Yes, ma'am," "No, ma'am," "Yes, ma'am."

Finally me and Howard finished and, I swear, you couldn't hardly even see that trap nestled there in the bushes. I ran inside the house and got the pie tin of table scraps I'd been saving. A piece of bacon. A biscuit. Some tuna noodle casserole. I pushed the pie tin way back up into the corner of the trap and said, "Okay, now all we have to do is wait."

Twelve

Me and Howard waited and waited but Wishbone never showed up. Gus had come outside a couple of times and sat with us, chewing on a toothpick and stroking the scrawny black cat curled up in his lap. Every now and then, Bertha would stick her head out of the front door and call out, "Catch him yet?"

We'd put our fingers to our lips and shush her and she'd slap her hand over her mouth and go, "Oops. Sorry."

When the sun began to disappear behind the mountains and the lightning bugs twinkled out in the garden, Gus stood up in that slow way of his and said, "Want me to drive you home, Howard?"

"No, sir," Howard said. "I'll walk."

I wondered if Gus was thinking what I was. That it was liable to take him all night to get home with that up-down walk of his. But Gus just stretched and said, "All righty, then," and ambled off toward the house.

"See you," Howard said, and headed up the driveway toward the road.

I sat there by the trap and looked over at Gus and Bertha's little house nestled on the side of the mountain. How come Bertha hadn't told me Mama had been here? Had Mama liked it here? Had she picked pole beans out in the garden with Gus? Had she helped Bertha make bread-and-butter pickles? Had she sat on the porch at night, gazing up at Pegasus? Had she slept in that room with those canning jars?

Finally I got up and went inside. I looked around the living room at Gus's old easy chair, the dusty table covered with magazines and coffee cups, the TV with a bowl of plastic fruit on top. Had Mama sat in that chair? Propped her feet on that table while she watched soap operas on that TV?

I could hear Gus and Bertha out on the porch talking. Every now and then, Bertha's laughter danced through the screen door. Finally I went out there and sat in the lawn chair next to them. Light from the kitchen sent a soft glow over the porch. I took a deep breath and said, "So, Mama came here one time, right?"

The two of them looked at each other. Gus cleared his throat and shifted in his seat. Bertha reached over and put her hand on my arm.

"Yes, she did," she said.

"Oh." I watched one of the cats swatting a moth that was flitting around the porch. "When?"

"A long time ago," Bertha said.

"But when?"

"When you were just a baby," she said.

"So I came, too?"

From somewhere down in the woods, a bullfrog croaked, sending an echo across the mountains. Below us, crickets chirped in the tangled weeds under the porch.

Bertha gave me a sad-eyed look. "No," she said. "You didn't come."

"What about Jackie?" I said. "Did she come?"

"No, Jackie didn't come either."

"But where were me and Jackie?" I asked. "And Scrappy? What about him?"

Bertha leaned over closer to me. She smelled like talcum powder. "Charlie," she said. "Your mama came here and left you and Jackie and Scrappy behind. Showed up on my doorstep in the middle of the night with a garbage bag full of clothes."

"Did she just come to visit?" I asked. But in my heart, I knew the answer to that question.

"No, Charlie," Bertha said. "She just up and left y'all without looking back." Bertha's voice suddenly had an edge to it. Sharp and angry sounding. I would've never guessed Bertha could sound angry like that.

"Oh," I said.

Bertha continued, her voice getting sharper and angrier. "When I asked her what in the world she was doing running off like that, she looked me right in the eye and said, 'I'm tired of my old life. I'm startin' a new one.'"

A flash of heat lightning lit up the sky over the mountains and there was a low rumble of thunder.

"Then what happened?" I asked.

Bertha let out a big sigh. "Her new life didn't last too long."

"How long?"

"A couple of months."

"But what happened?"

"I told her what I thought about her new life and I reckon she didn't like it. She didn't want to hear what I thought about a mama who up and leaves her children behind. She stormed out of here like a freight train and hightailed it back to her old life and I haven't seen her since."

Another rumble of thunder echoed across the valley below us.

"I tried to call but she wouldn't even talk to me," Bertha said. "I sent you and Jackie cards and gifts but she sent 'em right back. After a while, I gave up." She patted my knee. "I'm sorry to tell you these things, Charlie."

I shrugged like it was no big deal but my quivering chin must've given me away. Bertha knelt in front of me and took both my hands in hers and said, "Your mama loves you very much, Charlie. But sometimes, she just loses her way."

Loses her way? I'd be happy to draw her a map to show her the way back to being my mama again.

I stared out into the dark woods below us and sent my laser thoughts zipping through the trees and over the creek and down into the streets of town to wherever Wishbone was. I wanted him to know how much I needed him and what a great life he would have with me. And I didn't even care one bit if Mama had a hissy fit about him.

"I wonder if Wishbone will come get that food in the trap tonight," I said.

"He'd be a dern fool dog if he didn't," Gus said. "And something tells me that dog is no fool, Butterbean."

This time, when he called me Butterbean, instead of feeling like a baby, I felt a tiny smile tugging at the corners of my mouth even though my insides were twisted up knowing my mama had just up and left me like that.

Then I said good night and went back to my room. I sat by the window and watched the heat lightning. Where was Wishbone? Chasing somebody's chickens? Fighting with that little black dog down by those trailers? Or maybe he was out there in that trap this very minute eating tuna noodle casserole.

I climbed into bed and thought about Mama. What was her new life supposed to be? Was she going to stay here in Colby forever? Was she going to be a school-teacher or a librarian or maybe open a beauty parlor down there on Black Mountain Road? Was she going to find a new husband who didn't fight so much? Was she going to have new kids and give them cake with pink and purple flowers when they got home from school?

But what was the use of thinking about that? She had gone back to her old life and there she is and here I am, with my family all broken and scattered every which way.

Outside, the rain had started, slow and soft at first and then faster and louder. The wind picked up and blew cool and damp through the screen. Suddenly I sat up, my heart pounding. I hadn't made my wish today! My mind raced, thinking about my list of things to wish on. Too late for stars. No ladybugs in here. No four-leaf clovers or pennies or dandelions. And then I couldn't believe what happened next. From far off in the trees outside the window came the song of a mockingbird. Hearing a bird sing in the rain is on my list of things to make a wish on. So I closed my eyes and made my wish.

Thirteen

And so my life in Colby, North Carolina, marched on. Rumbling down the mountain on the school bus beside Howard. Ignoring those hillbilly kids who wouldn't give me the time of day. Playing Bible Detective at church. Waiting for Wishbone to eat hot dogs from the pie tin. Gazing up at the stars on the porch with Gus and Bertha. Making my wish every day.

Jackie called every once in a while to tell me about her happy life back in Raleigh. She was going to the prom with that boy Arlo. She and Carol Lee might work at the Waffle House this summer. She got a fake tattoo of a butterfly on her ankle.

I told her about Wishbone and how he was going to be mine and she asked me if I really thought that was a good idea. I told her, yes, it was a very good idea and that was that.

I'd seen Wishbone three more times. Sniffing at trash in the parking lot of the Dairy Freeze. Trotting along Highway 14 in the rain. Eating something out of a paper bag under a picnic table beside Brushy Creek.

Twice I'd found the pie tin in the trap empty but I hadn't seen him anywhere nearby. Luckily, there were only two more weeks of school left and then I would have my days free to spend more time by the trap, but I was beginning to worry that Wishbone was never going to be mine. Maybe I was wasting my time even thinking about it.

"I heard Wishbone barking last night," Howard said one day while we sat on the old couch on his front porch eating Popsicles.

"How do you know it was him?" I asked, watching Cotton jumping onto a milk crate in the yard with orange Popsicle juice running down his chin and onto his bare stomach.

"I just know," Howard said.

"We're never gonna catch him," I said. "Gus was right. He likes being a stray."

"Don't be a quitter," Howard said.

"I'm not a quitter."

"Yes, you are."

I stamped my foot. "I am not!"

Howard licked melted Popsicle off the side of his hand and said, "Pineapple."

I flopped back against the sofa and hurled my Popsicle stick out into the yard. That pineapple plan of his was starting to get on my nerves.

"Oh, good gravy, Charlie," he said. "Don't be a baby."

"I'm not a baby!" I hollered.

Howard shrugged. "You sure are acting like one," he said.

Just then Mrs. Odom came out on the porch, wiping her hands on a dish towel. But my temper had a hold on me and I could *not* shake it. I also could not stop myself from yelling, "Well, at least I'm not a squirrel-eating hillbilly like you."

Then I stomped down the steps, marched across the yard, climbed on Lenny's bike, and raced up the road toward Gus and Bertha's. When I got there, I dropped the bike in the yard and headed for the house. But as I reached the front door, I heard something over by the trap. I turned to look and couldn't believe my eyes. Wishbone was in there gobbling up meat loaf and french fries.

I didn't waste one more second. I raced across the yard and slammed the door of the trap shut with a bang. Wishbone let out a yelp and jumped clear up off the ground. Then he slinked back into the corner and hung his head, dragging his ears on the ground. He looked so scared it like to broke my heart.

"Hey, Wishbone," I whispered.

He pushed against that chicken wire so hard I was afraid he might bust right through it.

"I got more meat loaf," I said.

He cocked his head.

"Wait right here," I said. "I'll be back."

I closed the latch on the door of the trap and hurried inside the house, calling for Bertha. We nearly collided when I darted into the kitchen.

She clutched her heart and said, "Charlie! Lordy! You scared the dickens out of me."

"I got him!" I hollered. "I got Wishbone!"

I yanked the refrigerator door open and took out a foil-wrapped slice of meat loaf and ran back out to the yard. Bertha ran after me, calling, "I knew it! I knew my meat loaf would do the trick."

When we got to the trap, Wishbone was digging at the ground beside the wire like he was trying to dig a hole clear through to China. Dirt and pebbles flew out behind him. When he saw us, he stopped and backed up into the far corner of the trap again.

I unwrapped the foil. "I brought you more meat loaf," I said.

He let out a little whine, soft and pitiful. I could hear Bertha telling me to be careful and don't stick my fingers through the chicken wire and stuff like that. But I kept my eyes on Wishbone and told him not to be scared. Then I stuck a piece of meat loaf through the wire near him and waited.

His nose twitched as the meat loaf smell drifted his way. He stood up and sniffed some more.

"Come on, Wishbone," I said. "It's for you."

He took one step forward, keeping his eyes on the meat loaf. He took another step and then another till he was right at my hand. Then he snatched that meat loaf, swallowed it in one gulp, and wagged his tail.

Wag.

Wag.

Wag.

Three tiny wags like he was thanking me.

I turned to Bertha. "Did you see that?" I asked.

Bertha nodded. "I sure did. I confess I thought you

were going to lose a finger or two." She reached into the pocket of her apron and pulled out two saltine crackers. "Give him these," she said.

I gave Wishbone the crackers, and after he gobbled them up, he looked at me and wagged his tail again.

Then Bertha helped me look for the collar Gus had made from an old leather belt of his. We got rope from the garden shed and tied it to the collar. I ran back inside and got more food. Some cereal. A piece of raisin bread. A couple of slices of bologna.

Then I raced back out to the trap with Bertha not far behind, calling, "Wait for me!"

Fourteen

Wishbone didn't like that collar one bit. He bucked like a bronco when I put it on him, flinging his head this way and that. Then he sat down and dug his feet in like a mule when I pulled on the rope to get him out of the trap. But after leaving a trail of bologna like Hansel and Gretel's bread crumbs, I managed to get him to follow me, step by step, to the house. Once we were inside, Bertha locked the screen door and I untied the rope. Then we sat on the sofa and watched him.

He sniffed everything that was worth sniffing in that house. The shaggy green rug by the front door. Gus's easy chair. Bertha's basket of yarn. Then he made his way cautiously through the rest of the house, inspecting the coatrack by the back door, licking crumbs off the linoleum floor under the kitchen table. When he spied one of the cats up on the windowsill, he let out a bark. The cat arched his back and hissed. I was relieved when Wishbone just walked away. Bertha had been worried that he was going to chase the cats, and I have to admit I had worried about that a little bit, too.

After a while, he got tired of sniffing and laid down next to the sofa and went to sleep. I tiptoed over and sat beside him, stroking his fur and whispering his name. I couldn't hardly believe I had my very own dog.

When Gus got home that night, he seemed pleased as punch to see Wishbone sitting there in the kitchen while Bertha cooked chicken fried steak and black-eyed peas.

"Well, don't that beat all?" he said.

I couldn't keep my hands off of Wishbone. I petted his head and stroked his ears and scratched his belly.

"Isn't he something?" I said.

Gus nodded. "He sure is."

"He smells like something, too," Bertha said, making a face. "You're gonna have to give him a good bath out in the yard tomorrow."

"I will."

Tomorrow was Saturday, so I had all day to spend with him. I'd bathe him and walk him. Maybe I'd teach him a trick, like to sit or lay down. I might even take him to Howard's house if I decided not to be mad at him anymore for calling me a quitter and a baby. And then I remembered calling him a squirrel-eating hillbilly with Mrs. Odom standing right there on the porch. My stomach squeezed up and my face burned just thinking about that. I knew Howard wouldn't be mad 'cause that was his way. But I bet Mrs. Odom hated me now. I bet she wouldn't want me in her house messing up their goodness with my hateful words.

That night, I took Wishbone out on the porch with us. Every now and then, he perked his ears up at the sound of a rabbit or something rustling down in the woods. But eventually, he laid down and rested his chin right on top of my foot. He didn't even pay any mind to the cats strolling around him.

"I think you got yourself a good one, Charlie," Gus said.

I smiled down at Wishbone. "I bet he'll be as good as Skeeter," I said.

Gus nodded. "I bet he will."

"You know what I like best about dogs?" Bertha said.

Gus and I waited.

"They love you no matter what." Bertha smiled down

at Wishbone. "Shoot, I know folks who are cranky or stuck up or bold-faced liars and their dogs love 'em like they're saints or something. Know what I mean?"

Gus nodded and said, "Yep."

"I hate to admit it," Bertha went on, "but I bet half these cats of mine would run off and never look back if somebody came along with a can of sardines."

I leaned down and ran my hand down Wishbone's side. His fur was soft and warm and he snored real soft while he slept. Then I gazed up at the starry sky and had a feeling I hadn't had in a long time. Thankful. I felt thankful that I had my very own dog who would love me no matter what.

When I woke up the next morning, the first thing I did was look for Wishbone to make sure I hadn't just dreamed he was mine. Sure enough, there he was, curled up on the floor beside me. I'd put one of my pillows there for him and he hadn't wasted one minute flopping down on it.

I spent the morning bathing him and combing him and picking burrs out of his tail and ticks off of his ears. I knew he didn't like it much but he let me do it. When I was done, he looked so handsome and smelled so good that Bertha kept making a fuss over him and running back into the house to get him another chicken liver. He was so skinny you could count his ribs right through his fur.

"We need to fatten him up," Bertha said.

After lunch, I practiced walking him with the rope tied to his collar. At first, he'd made it clear that he didn't like it. He'd jerk his head this way and that or sit down and refuse to budge. But I kept a plastic bag full of tiny pieces of cheese and bacon and stuff to lure him along, and after a while, he was trotting right beside me. Around the yard. Through the garden. Up the driveway and back.

I let him take a nap tied up in the shade of the big oak tree on the steep slope by the back porch. Bertha brought a tablecloth outside and spread it on the ground next to him. Then the two of us had pimiento cheese sandwiches and sweet tea for lunch. Bertha told me a story about some old man named Cooter who used to be the mayor of Colby.

"He carried a gun," she said. "And if anybody parked in front of Town Hall where they weren't supposed to, he'd shoot their tires out."

"Really?"

"Really. And his wife used to wash her underpants and hang 'em on the antenna of her car and then drive around town till they were dry."

I wrinkled my nose and said, "Eww."

Bertha laughed. "I know! That big ole underwear looked like the national flag of the Land of Big Behinds flapping in the breeze like that."

Me and Bertha had a good laugh over that. Every now and then, Wishbone's feet jerked and he let out a little yip while he slept. I wondered if he was dreaming about running free again without a rope tied to him. I hoped not.

I took a gulp of sweet tea and watched the honeybees flitting over the clover beside us.

Clover! Maybe I could find a four-leaf clover. So while Bertha told me about how Cooter and his wife bought a gold mine in Nevada and moved away, I searched and searched. Sure enough, I found one. But I didn't pick it. If you pick it, it will bring you good luck, but if you leave it growing there, you can make a wish, which is exactly what I did.

After lunch I decided I wasn't mad at Howard anymore, so I tied Wishbone's rope-leash to the handlebars of Lenny's bike and pedaled down the road to the Odoms'. Wishbone seemed to love that, racing along beside me with his ears flapping and his tongue hanging out.

When I got to Howard's, he and Dwight and Cotton were in the front yard playing some game that involved throwing tin cans and punching each other.

"Hey, y'all!" I called. "Look what I got!"

They raced over and gathered around Wishbone, stroking his back and patting his head.

"Wow, Charlie," Howard said. "You did it!"

I couldn't stop myself from beaming at him. "I know!" I said. "And isn't he great?"

Howard scratched behind Wishbone's ears. "Looks like he's got some beagle in him," he said. "I like his ears."

While the Odom boys made a fuss over him, Wishbone sat there with his eyes closed and a doggy smile on his face.

We played with him the whole afternoon. Cotton kept tossing popcorn for him to catch and Dwight led him across the yard on the leash and got him to jump up onto an old cooler and sit. Howard even taught him to shake hands in no time flat.

"He's smart!" Howard said, and we all nodded in agreement.

"Let's show Mama his tricks," Howard said, hurrying to the porch in his up-down way.

With everybody making such a fuss over Wishbone, I'd forgotten about what I'd said yesterday when my Scrappy temper had grabbed hold of me. But when Mrs. Odom came out to the yard to see Wishbone, I remembered. My face burned and I couldn't even look at her.

Howard showed her how Wishbone could sit on the cooler and shake hands.

"Ain't he smart?" he said.

"He is smart, for sure," Mrs. Odom said. "And lucky he's found such a fine friend as Charlie."

I felt relief wash over me. Maybe Mrs. Odom wasn't mad at me, after all.

"Let's get some treats and teach him to roll over," Howard said.

"That's a good idea." Mrs. Odom ruffled my hair. "I've got some squirrel pie fresh out of the oven."

I wanted to sink right into the ground when she said that. Or disappear into thin air. Poof! Gone. But of course I couldn't, so I just stood there with my face burning and my stomach in a knot.

Dwight and Cotton hooted and hollered, slapping their knees and saying, "Squirrel pie?"

Mrs. Odom put her arm around my shoulder, and

when I got up my courage to look at her, she winked at me. "I'm so glad to have a feisty female around here to help me keep these boys under control. I been needing a girl on my team."

On her team? Mrs. Odom needed me on her team?

I wished I could've saved that moment there in that weed-filled yard surrounded by those good-hearted Odoms, with Wishbone sitting there on the cooler in front of us. Just pack it into one of Bertha's canning jars to keep in my room. Then when I was feeling bad about myself or loaded down with all my troubles, I could open it up and breathe in the goodness of it and I'd feel better.

But the moment passed, and Howard brought a piece of chicken out to the yard and we tried to teach Wishbone to roll over, but all he wanted to do was eat that chicken.

"Back in Raleigh, we've got a fence around our yard, so he can run free back there," I said.

Howard's smile faded and he said, "Do you think your mama will let you keep him?"

Shoot! I wished he hadn't said that 'cause it stirred my worries up and I'd been doing such a good job of keeping them locked in tight. The truth of the matter was, there was no telling what Mama would think about me showing up back there with Wishbone. But I managed to push that worry away and say, "Sure she will. She's gonna love him."

"When are you leaving?" Howard asked in a tiny, quivery voice.

I shrugged. "I don't know," I said. "Soon, I bet." But I knew in my heart that Mama still didn't have her feet on the ground. I mean, I hadn't even gotten so much as a postcard or a phone call from her since I'd been in Colby. I knew she was still laying around in her bathrobe in the dark, drinking diet soda for supper and not thinking about me one bit.

Howard got quiet after that, so I finally tied Wishbone to the bike and headed back up to Gus and Bertha's. When I got there, Gus was sitting at the kitchen table while Bertha sliced green peppers from the garden and jabbered about that fancy new drugstore they were building out on Route 26.

"Well, *there* they are," Gus said when he saw me and Wishbone. "A girl and her dog." Then he reached in his pocket and pulled out something that he held out to me in his palm. A little bone-shaped dog tag with *Wishbone* engraved on it. He turned it over and showed me it had a phone number on the other side.

"Gus!" Bertha squealed. "You are a prince." She kissed his cheek. "Ain't he a prince, Charlie?"

I nodded.

"Then I might be a king when you take a look at that," Gus said, nodding toward the coatrack by the back door. Hanging there with the raincoats and cardigans was a red dog leash.

"I figured he needed a real leash instead of that ole rope," Gus said.

Bertha kissed him again. "Now you are a king," she said. "Ain't he, Charlie?"

I just couldn't get over Gus going and doing such a nice thing for me. "Yes, ma'am," I agreed. "He is."

Then Gus took Wishbone's collar off, attached the little tag to it, and put it back on. When I looked down at him with his collar on and his very own tag with his very own name, he seemed like he'd been mine forever. Like he belonged right here with me, not a stray anymore.

And in the middle of that happy moment, I had a tiny seed of a thought that I hurried to push out of my mind before it had time to grow. That thought was this: Where in the world do *I* belong?

Fifteen

The next day before Sunday school, I raced to the fellowship hall where that Garden of Blessings was up on the bulletin board. I searched the paper flowers until I found mine. The other kids had made a bunch of flowers 'cause I guess they had a bunch of blessings. But I had only made one and for my blessing, I had written, "I am healthy," because Audrey had written that on one of hers. I took my flower down and with a purple crayon I added, "I have a dog named Wishbone."

When I got to Sunday school, I tried to tell kids about my new dog, but it seemed like nobody cared. They were busy calling out sins for Mrs. Mackey to write on a blackboard.

Cussing.

Bullying.

Lying.

Disobeying your parents.

The sins were flying around that room like blackbirds in a cornfield.

"Charlie," Mrs. Mackey said. "Can you think of a sin?"

I bet leaving your children behind so you can start a new life is a sin. But, of course, I wasn't about to add that one to the list, so I just said, "No, ma'am."

"What about *kicking* and *shoving*?" Audrey said.

Then Howard started muttering under his breath next to me, "Pineapple. Pineapple. Pineapple."

And maybe it was because we were in church, but a miracle happened. I was able to push my temper down and put a lid on it. I smiled and clamped my mouth shut tight so I wouldn't say anything to ruin this miracle moment. And then another miracle floated through that Sunday school window and settled on my shoulder and nudged me to say, "I shouldn't have kicked and shoved you like I did, Audrey. I'm sorry."

Well, let me tell you, that took the wind right out of her sails. Her eyebrows shot up and her mouth dropped open and then she said, "That's okay."

After Sunday school, on our way to the fellowship hall, Howard slapped me on the back and said, "Good job, Charlie. I told you that pineapple trick would work."

I'd been counting the minutes until the last day of school. When it finally came, I skipped up to the bus stop in Jackie's majorette boots. I didn't care that they were hot and rubbed blisters on my heels. I strutted up the aisle of the bus and winked at those giggling girls like Jackie'd told me to do.

"Just wink at 'em," she had said on the phone one night. "That'll throw 'em for a loop and they won't know *what* to do."

But some of those girls still giggled when I dropped into the seat next to Howard and handed him one of Bertha's banana muffins.

"Thanks," he said. Then he broke it in half and started picking out the raisins, placing them in a little pile on the seat between us.

"Wishbone dug up some beans last night," I said.

"Uh-oh." Howard took a bite of muffin and made a face. Then he fished a raisin out of his mouth and added it to the pile on the seat. "Gus get mad?" he asked.

"Naw. He just said I couldn't let him in the garden anymore."

"Bertha get mad?"

I shook my head. "She told me a story about her cousin's dog who ate corn right off the stalks in her grandaddy's garden and got so sick he almost died."

As the bus made its way down the mountain, I thought about my old school back in Raleigh. It felt like I'd been in Colby forever and I hadn't heard from a single one of my so-called friends back home, except Carlene Morgan. She had sent me a postcard with a picture of the capitol building where my class had gone on a field trip.

You are lucky you didn't have to go, she had written. *It was boring. LOL.*

Jackie told me she had seen my best friend, Alvina, at the movies with some girls from our Girl Scout troop.

"Did she ask about me?" I said.

"No, but I told her you were doing good," Jackie said.

Doing good?

Ha!

How would Jackie know? She was too busy living her perfect life with Carol Lee to think about me. She hardly ever even called anymore.

One time when I was in third grade, I went with Scrappy to the cemetery to see where his daddy was buried. We found the moss-covered headstone that read: *Albert Eugene Reese*. At the top, it said *Gone but Not Forgotten*. I wasn't even laying under the cold hard ground like Albert, but I was gone *and* forgotten.

Bertha kept telling me I should invite some of my old friends from Raleigh to visit me this summer. I didn't want to hurt her feelings, but that sounded like a bad idea to me. What would we do? Watch the squash grow out in the garden? Stare at Pegasus on the porch all night? Where would they sleep? Squished in my little bed with me on my Cinderella pillows? No, those Raleigh girls would not have fun here in Colby.

When the last bell of the day rang, I couldn't get out of there fast enough. Every day I had counted the minutes until I could get back home to Wishbone. Bertha told me he stood at the door and whined for me when I was gone. "That's the truth," she said. "Cross my heart and hope to die."

On the way up the mountain, I stared out the window while Howard told me about Burl buying a motorcycle and his mama being mad as all get-out.

Then guess what? I saw three birds perched together

up on the telephone line along the side of the road. Three birds on a wire was on my list of things to wish on. But it has to be exactly three birds according to Scrappy's friend Ray, and that's not as easy as it sounds. So I made my wish quick before one of them flew away.

Sixteen

"Guess what?" Bertha said when I got home. She reached into the pocket of her apron and pulled out an envelope. "You got a letter from your daddy!"

"I did?" I stared at the envelope in her hand. That was Scrappy's handwriting all right. Giant wiggly printing, like a first grader wrote it.

I put Wishbone's leash on and took him out front. I sat in Gus's lawn chair by the garden and stared down at the envelope.

Miss Charlie Reese

If Mama had sent me a letter (which she never would) she would have written *Miss Charlemagne Reese* to aggravate me. Then she would probably tell me good-bye because she was starting her new life without me.

I studied the envelope some more. *Wake County Correctional Center* was printed in the corner.

Well, now, that didn't sound nearly as bad as *county jail*. I think folks in the county jail have to stay for a long time. But if Scrappy was just getting corrected, maybe that wouldn't take too long.

I sniffed the envelope to see if I could smell his after-shave, but I couldn't. I took out the folded notebook paper and smoothed it on my lap.

Dear Charlie,

It's your old Scrappy pappy here saying hello and how are you?

I am fine.

This place is okay except for the lumpy gravy and lousy pillow.

Jackie came to visit and brought me Hershey bars and toothpaste.

I bet you are having fun with Gus and Bertha. Tell them I will send some money when I can.

Love,

Scrappy

I turned the paper over to see if there was more on the back.

Nope.

That was it.

I looked at the word *love*. I traced the letters with my finger. Then I folded the paper up and put it back in the envelope.

The next day, I was bored by lunchtime. I'd practiced sit and stay with Wishbone. I'd helped Bertha inspect the okra to figure out how many jars we'd need for pickling. I'd looked for four-leaf clovers over by the back porch, but I didn't find one. Then I'd shared my peanut butter sandwich with Wishbone, and that was it. Nothing else to do.

So I figured I'd ride Lenny's bike down to Howard's. I hooked Wishbone's leash on the handlebars and off we went.

When I got there, the Odoms' house was buzzing like a beehive. Cotton was making something with sticks and rocks in the small square of shade next to the porch. Burl and Lenny were over in the driveway peering at the engine of Burl's motorcycle. Every now and then, one of them would bang on something with a wrench. Dwight was tossing a basketball into the hoop on the streetlight pole at the edge of the yard. And Howard? I couldn't believe what he was doing. A crossword puzzle! Sitting on that ratty couch on the porch doing a crossword puzzle. What kind of kid does that on the first day of summer?

"Hey," he said, adjusting his glasses.

Wishbone jumped on the couch next to him and flopped over on his side, panting.

"Hey." I lifted the hair off the back of my neck and fanned myself. "It sure is hot," I said.

"Wanna study for Bible Detective?" Howard asked.

Bible Detective?

I almost said, "Are you nuts?" but for once I managed to keep my thoughts to myself and I said, "No, not really."

"I'll give you some of my Bible bucks," he said.

I shook my head. "That's okay."

"Then what do you want to do?"

I shrugged. "I got a letter from Scrappy," I said.

Howard sat up straight. "You did?" He put the crossword puzzle on the couch beside us. "From jail?"

"It's not jail," I said. "It's a correctional facility."

"Same thing," Howard said.

"It is not!"

"I'm pretty sure it is."

"It is *not*!" I said so loud Wishbone's head shot up and he looked at me like I was crazy.

Pineapple.

Pineapple.

Pineapple.

I did *not* want to get mad at Howard on the first day of summer.

I must admit that even though me and Howard hadn't known each other very long, he could read me like a book. I could tell he knew I was wrestling with that temper of mine again, 'cause he changed the subject and just said, "Well, that's good that you got a letter." He scratched Wishbone behind the ear. "What'd he say?"

I wanted to tell Howard that Scrappy said how much he misses me and he can't wait to come home and watch *Wheel of Fortune* with me again. That he was gonna cook up a fancy supper for Mama with candles on the table and Willie Nelson on the radio and maybe she'd wear that red dress he loved so much. And that when Jackie got her driver's license, he was gonna let her drive all of us out to the country to buy corn and strawberries at a farm stand by the side of the road. Then we'd go home and have a barbecue out in the yard. And we might even hold hands and say the blessing like Howard's family did. But I didn't tell him any of that. I told him the truth.

"He said they have lumpy gravy and lousy pillows," I said.

"That's too bad."

I almost told him that Scrappy signed his letter with the word *love*, but then, that would probably sound dumb to a boy who gets loved so much every day of his life.

"Hey, maybe Mama will help us make cookies to send to him sometime."

"Really?"

"Sure," Howard said. "Wanna go down to the creek?"

"Okay."

So me and Howard and Wishbone went behind the garage and followed the narrow trail that snaked through the cool, damp woods. I loved the earthy, mossy smell of the air and the soft tickle of the ferns that bowed down along the edges of the path. Wishbone trotted beside me, stopping every now and then to sniff at a tree or root around in a pile of rotten leaves. I wondered if he had been on this trail before. I bet he knew these woods better than anybody. Maybe he'd even slept under these very trees.

I wanted to take his leash off and let him run free, but I was scared to. What if he decided he'd had enough of me and ran off to be a stray again?

When we got to the creek, Wishbone nearly pulled me in when he jumped into the clear, gurgling water. Howard and I took off our shoes and stepped from rock to rock while Wishbone leaped and pranced, sending up splashes of cold mountain water.

"This feels good," I said.

"I know." Howard teetered on the slippery rocks and I was sure he was going to fall in any minute, but he didn't. Wishbone let out the funniest yips and bit at the water, trying to grab the tiny minnows that darted around the rocks.

"Look at him!" we both said at the exact same time.

I jumped off the rock to the edge of the creek and motioned for Howard. "Come quick," I hollered. "Hook pinkies."

"What?"

"Hook pinkies," I said. "We *both* get to wish."

"We do?"

I nodded. "If two people say the same thing at the exact same time, they hook pinkies and make a wish," I said. "Jackie taught me that."

So Howard jumped to the edge of the creek and we hooked pinkies. I closed my eyes and made my wish.

"Did you make a wish?" I asked.

"No."

"Why not?"

He stooped to swish his hand in the water, making the minnows scurry away. "I don't really have anything to wish for," he said.

I shook my head. How could anybody not have something to wish for? I mean, even if you just wished you didn't have a wart on your thumb or that you didn't have to eat oatmeal for breakfast, it seemed to me like you could think of *something* to wish for.

"Oh, good grief, Howard," I said. "There must be *something*."

"Well, actually, there *is* something I could wish for," he said.

So we hooked pinkies again and Howard closed his eyes.

"Did you make a wish?" I asked.

"Yep."

"I bet I know what it is."

"I can't tell or it won't come true. Remember?"

"No, *you* can't tell," I said. "But *I* can. It doesn't matter if I tell."

I didn't know for sure if that was true, but I think it probably was.

"Just don't say whether I'm right or not," I said.

"Okay."

"You wished you didn't have that up-down walk," I said.

When those words left my mouth, I could practically see them hurtling through the air toward Howard, quick and sharp, like razors.

Howard's face turned pale as a ghost and his eyes flicked down at the ground.

What had I done?

Why had I said that?

More than anything, I wanted to take those sharp words back, but I knew I couldn't.

It suddenly felt like everything was frozen in time. Just stopped cold, dead still. Like the creek water stopped flowing and the birds stopped chirping. Like the clouds above us stopped floating over the mountaintops. Even Wishbone stood still as a statue beside me.

Then Howard broke through that frozen curtain of time by grabbing his shoes and heading off up the path toward his house, leaving me standing there ashamed and heavyhearted.

I sat on the edge of the creek and held myself a pity party. That's what Jackie calls it when I feel sorry for myself.

"For heaven's sake, Charlie," she says, "stop having such a pity party."

But I couldn't help it. Why had I gone and said something so mean to the only kid in Colby who was nice to me? The kid who wanted to give me some of his Bible bucks and send cookies to Scrappy. The kid who let me share my troubles with him.

I pictured my clothesline full of troubles and saw myself pinning on another one. I stayed there by the creek wallowing in my pity, thinking about how this day had turned out so bad. But then, things suddenly went from bad to worse. A tiny striped chipmunk darted out of a rotten log beside the creek and Wishbone bolted after it, yanking the leash right out of my hand. And before I could even get myself up off the ground, he had disappeared into the woods.

Seventeen

I searched those woods till it was almost dark. I called Wishbone's name till my throat hurt. I walked up and down the side of the road till my legs ached. Finally I went to Howard's to get Lenny's bike that I left in the yard that afternoon. I could hear the Odoms inside eating supper, everybody laughing and saying "Pass the butter" and stuff. I pictured them in there crowded around the kitchen table. The boys poking each other and grabbing for the last biscuit. Mrs. Odom cooking up more fried chicken and kissing the tops of their heads. Mr. Odom's eyes twinkling as he watched his happy family. I wondered if Howard had told them what I said about his wish. And if he did, what did all those good-hearted Odoms think of me now?

When I got home, I went straight back to my room and held the biggest pity party of my life. I laid on Wishbone's pillow on the floor beside the bed, breathing in his doggy smell, and I cried until I fell asleep.

I woke up to Bertha whispering my name. The room was dark except for the faint glow of the lamp in the living room floating through the half-open door of my room.

I closed my eyes real quick and pretended like I was still asleep. I couldn't stand the thought of telling Bertha about my day. How Wishbone didn't want to be my dog anymore and had run off. How I had said such a mean thing to Howard.

I thought maybe Bertha would leave, but she didn't. She gave me a little shake and whispered my name again.

"Come get some supper," she said.

"I'm not hungry," I mumbled into the pillow.

"Your favorite," she said. "Grits with cheese and bacon."

I shook my head. I felt like a pouty baby. I even had the urge to suck my thumb. When I acted like this back in Raleigh, Mama would say, "Quit that baby whining before I jerk a knot in you."

But Bertha said, "You know, sometimes when you've

had a bad day, eating grits makes you feel better." She poked me with an elbow. "I know that from experience," she added.

I sat up and hugged my knees. I leaned a little closer to Bertha until we were touching. Arm to arm. Knee to knee. She smelled like someone who spent her days in the kitchen. Bacon and coffee and cinnamon. But she looked like someone who spent her days outdoors. Arms tan and leathery. Dirt under her fingernails.

"Wishbone is gone," I whispered.

She nodded and pushed a strand of wispy hair behind her ear. "Gus is out there looking for him," she said. "And Gus is a man you can count on."

A teeny-tiny glimmer of feel-better worked its way into my heart. I knew she was right about that. Gus did seem like a man you could count on.

"But what if Wishbone wants to be a stray again?" I asked.

Bertha sat up straight and took my chin in her hand. "Charlie Reese," she said. "You think that dog don't know a good thing when he sees one?"

"What good thing?" I said in my pouty baby voice.

She held up a finger each time she counted off. "One, he eats bologna for breakfast. Two, he sleeps on a pillow. And three, he is loved by an angel."

Angel?

Ha!

So here's where I had to go and ruin that image of me as an angel. "I said something mean to Howard," I muttered.

Silence.

Why had I gone and told her that? I wished I could take those words back. Gather them up like butterflies in a net. Stay an angel in her eyes.

And then I got this bad thought. What if Bertha was wrong about dogs loving you no matter what? What if Wishbone knows I'm mean and that's why he ran off?

I could feel Bertha's warm skin against mine. Hear her soft breathing in the stillness of that little room. Finally she slapped a hand on my knee and said, "You need some grits."

As soon as I woke up the next day, I looked down at the pillow on the floor and more than anything I wanted Wishbone to be there.

He wasn't.

I hurried into the kitchen. Bertha was shelling peas at the table.

"Where's Gus?" I asked.

"He went to work."

I sank into the chair across from her. "I guess he didn't find Wishbone," I said.

She looked at me all sad-eyed and shook her head. "No, he didn't. But he said to tell you we can get out there and look when he gets home. He set up that trap of yours last night and I put some scraps in it, so we can keep an eye on that. And don't forget Wishbone has a tag on his collar. I'm sure somebody will call us when they find him." She pushed a box of cereal toward me. "Eat some breakfast."

But how could I eat with my stomach all balled up like it was? And then there was my other problem. Howard. What was I going to do about Howard?

Guilt was gnawing at my insides as I watched Bertha shelling those peas. Every now and then, she glanced up at me, and when she did, I had to look away real quick. There she was over there on the other side of the table thinking I was an angel, and here I was on my side feeling about as far from an angel as anybody could be.

"Aren't you going to ask me what mean thing I said to Howard?" I asked her.

She shook her head. "No, I'm not."

"How come?"

She tossed a handful of peas into the bowl and leaned toward me. "Charlie," she said. "You can't judge people for the mistakes they make. You judge them for how they fix those mistakes." She reached across the table and patted my hand. "Besides, you think I haven't ever said a word or two I wanted to snatch back?" She winked. "Just ask Gus if you don't believe me."

It was for sure Bertha had said a lot of words in her life, seeing as how she was such a talker. But I was pretty sure none of those words were mean, like mine. Mean and Bertha did *not* go together.

"Now why don't you get dressed and we'll figure out what to do about Wishbone," she said.

But before I could even think about how to start this sorry day, someone knocked on the front screen door, and imagine my surprise when I saw who it was. Howard!

I stood there barefoot in my pajamas with my hair a big rat's nest and searched for something to say. But then Bertha jumped right in and said, "Well, looky here who showed up on our doorstep, Charlie!" She held the door open. "Howard Odom in need of some cinnamon toast, I bet," she said. "Or cereal. Or eggs. Or grits. You need some grits, Howard?"

He stepped inside and shook his head. "No, ma'am."

Then he turned to me and said, "Wanna pick wild strawberries?" He held up an empty milk carton with the top cut off. "I know where there's tons."

"Um . . ." I pushed hair out of my eyes. "I . . . um . . ."

"Y'all go on and pick strawberries," Bertha said. "I'll keep an eye on things here." She nodded in the direction of the trap at the edge of the yard.

And then I collapsed into a puddle of sorrow on the couch and told Howard about Wishbone running off. When I finished, all I wanted to do was flop down and cry, but Howard said, "What are you sitting here for? Let's go find him!" Then the next thing I knew he was out the door and grabbing his bike, leaving me to run to my room to get dressed and scramble after him.

Eighteen

Me and Howard rode our bikes up and down that mountain road all morning long. We tromped through woods, pushing our way around thick shrubs and stepping over pricker bushes. We went back to the creek behind Howard's house three times, calling and whistling. We peered under porches and opened sheds and circled barns. By lunchtime, the blazing summer sun overhead left pockets of melted asphalt in the road and trickles of sweat down our backs.

We didn't talk much, and that was fine by me. I'd gone over and over in my head how I would say I'm sorry to Howard for what I'd said about his wish. But whenever I thought the time was right, my mouth went dry and my throat squeezed up and the words I'd planned to say stayed bottled up inside.

We went back to Gus and Bertha's a few times to check the trap, but the table scraps were still in the pie tin. We had lunch on Howard's front porch, sitting on the couch eating Vienna sausages and cold pork and beans off of paper plates on our laps. Dwight and Cotton were out in the yard throwing rocks at the mailbox. They hit the metal with a loud *thwang* and left little dents on the sides.

Mrs. Odom came out and told them to stop, and then she sat on the couch and told me not to worry. She was sure Wishbone would come back.

"You got to think positive," she said.

"Yes, ma'am," I mumbled.

Did she know I'd said that mean thing to Howard? If she knew, I bet she wouldn't want me on her team anymore.

That afternoon Burl drove us into town to search parking lots and Dumpsters. Dwight and Lenny made some Lost Dog signs and we nailed them to telephone poles and fence posts.

It was almost suppertime when me and Howard rode our bikes back to Gus and Bertha's and checked the trap one more time. Then we sat in lawn chairs out by the garden and watched dragonflies flit over the tops of the marigolds.

In my head, I said, "Howard, I'm sorry I said that about your wish. You know, about your up-down walk?"

Then I'd say, "Shoot, nobody even *cares* about your up-down walk."

But then, he'd know that was a big, fat lie, 'cause he saw those kids leaving him out of their kickball games and cutting in line in front of him like he was invisible.

So I sat there in silence with my thoughts spinning in my head. Maybe he didn't care about what I said. I mean, he was still being nice to me. He was helping me look for Wishbone.

"You sure do look forlorn," Howard said.

I didn't know one other kid in the whole world who would use the word *forlorn*. But that was the perfect word to describe me.

Forlorn.

Just before supper, Jackie called and told me she went to see Scrappy in jail and he got a tattoo.

"Don't you even want to know what it *is*?" she asked when I didn't say anything.

"Um, sure."

"A bird," she said. "A blackbird in a cage. Right on the back of his hand. Can you believe that?"

"I guess."

Then she rambled on about how graduating from high school wasn't all it's cracked up to be and how much she hated her job at the Waffle House.

"People leave the tables all nasty with syrup," she said. "And they plop their crying babies in a highchair and expect me to bring them their blueberry waffles in, like, a minute."

She told me that her boyfriend, Arlo, wrecked his car and turned out to be a loser.

"And Carol Lee saw him at the mall with Darla Jacobs," she said, "so I told him adios, sucker, and then—"

"Aren't you gonna ask me about Wishbone?" I said.

"What?"

I'd been telling her all about Wishbone when she called. How smart he is and how he learned to sit and stay and how he slept beside my bed.

"Wishbone," I said. "My dog. Aren't you even gonna ask me about him?"

"Oh, um, sure," she said. "How is Wishbone?"

"Gone!" I hollered. "He's gone." And then I spewed out the whole sorry story about how he'd run off and how I'd looked everywhere but I figured he'd rather be a stray than live with me. I tried to stop but I couldn't. I moved on to how he didn't want me the same as nobody else wanted me and how I hoped she was enjoying her perfect life while I was stuck here in Colby with a bunch of squirrel-eating hillbillies. And then I hung up and sat on the floor with my back against the wall. I could see Bertha in the kitchen stirring something on the stove and pretending like she hadn't heard me.

When the phone rang again, I just looked at it there in my hand.

Bertha stopped stirring.

Ring.

Ring.

Ring.

"Hello?" I said in a trembly voice.

"Charlie . . ." Jackie's voice floated through the telephone line, soft and sure. From Raleigh to Colby. I pictured that voice traveling from Carol Lee's fancy brick house, along highways and over treetops, and then up the winding roads and down the gravel driveway into this little house perched on the side of the mountain and finally getting to me, sitting on the floor and needing to hear it.

"I'm sorry about Wishbone," Jackie said. "I really am. I hope he comes back."

I watched a fly dart from the window screen to the lamp to the ceiling.

"Charlie?" Jackie said.

"What?"

"I know this whole situation has been hard on you." Situation?

Is that what this was? A situation?

"I think Mama's getting better," Jackie said. "I talked to her yesterday and she sounded better."

What did that mean? That she got out of bed? That she got her feet on the ground? That she cared one little bit about me? That I'd go back to Raleigh and our broken family would suddenly disappear and in its place would be a *real* family, holding hands and saying the blessing?

"Maybe I can come visit you soon," Jackie went on. "I'm gonna get my driver's license in a couple of weeks. Did I tell you that? And Carol Lee got a car for graduation. Can you believe that? If I get some time off from my godforsaken job I could come to Colby. We could go to Asheville and hang out. They have vegan restaurants there. Did you know that? I'm thinking about becoming vegan and I bet if I . . ."

She jabbered on about all the things we could do, but

she left out the part about how she would go back to her perfect life and I would still be here without my dog and wishing I hadn't been mean to Howard.

That night when Gus got home, the three of us drove around looking for Wishbone. We went down to the school and over to the diner. We drove through trailer parks and up alleys. While we drove, Bertha told us a story she'd read in the newspaper about a dog that fell out of the back of a van in North Carolina and managed to find his way back home to Indiana.

"Almost four hundred miles!" she said. "The family had been on vacation over in Maggie Valley. I can't hardly believe that."

Gus was quiet, shifting a toothpick from one side of his mouth to the other while he scanned the roadside and the parking lots and the woods as he drove. Every now and then he said, "Don't worry, Butterbean, we'll find him." But I was thinking that maybe now was the time to change my wish. Maybe next time I got a chance, I should wish my dog would come back.

Finally it got too dark to see much anymore, so we headed home. We turned into the driveway and that old car bounced and squeaked over the holes, the crunch of tires on gravel echoing in the still evening air. The headlights sent beams of light dancing through the mountain laurel and chokeberries beside the driveway.

Finally the house came into view and I thought my heart was going to leap right out of me at what I saw.

There was Wishbone, wagging his tail as he trotted toward us, dragging his leash on the ground behind him.

Nineteen

Wishbone had liverwurst and scrambled eggs for dinner every night for a week. He learned to roll over and turn in circles and flip a dog biscuit off his nose and catch it. And he didn't sleep on the floor beside my bed anymore. He slept right in the bed *with* me. I didn't mind his liverwurst breath one bit. I loved his soft, warm fur and the feel of his heartbeat against my cheek when I hugged him.

Every night after supper, when me and Gus and Bertha sat out on the porch, Wishbone snored contentedly while I rubbed my bare feet over his warm back. Sometimes he'd jump up and let out a bark at a noise down in the woods. A raccoon or a possum or maybe even just the rustle of leaves in the wind.

"That is one happy dog, Butterbean," Gus would say.

Then Bertha would urge Gus to tell us another story about his dog, Skeeter.

"How about that time he fell in the river when y'all were fishing and your brother jumped in after him and flipped the boat over?" she said.

Gus chuckled, but before he could say a word, Bertha said, "Oh, I know! Tell Charlie how your sister used to dress Skeeter up in her Girl Scout uniform."

I took Wishbone to the Odoms' almost every day. I still hadn't told Howard I was sorry for what I said about his up-down walk, so there was always a big ole elephant in the room for me. But Howard, he never let on that anything had happened between us. Still, I felt mad at myself for not speaking up. I kept thinking about what Bertha had said about judging folks for how they fix their mistakes, and I knew I wasn't doing a very good job of fixing mine.

Every time me and Wishbone showed up at the Odoms' front door, one of them would say hey and wave us in and I'd get caught up in the flurry of that family like a tornado spinning me off of my feet.

Me and Howard played Parcheesi at the kitchen table

with a fan whirring in the doorway, while Wishbone scurried around searching for dropped crackers or spilled juice. Cotton would stick his face right up against the fan and let out a Tarzan yell, his voice coming out all quivery and making us laugh.

Burl and Lenny would come in and make tomato sandwiches, leaving greasy black fingerprints on everything they touched. It seemed like they were always working on some kind of engine. Car. Motorcycle. Lawnmower. Every once in a while, a swear word would drift through the screen door from out in the yard and Mrs. Odom would march out there and tell them to hush up talking like that.

Dwight went to baseball camp at the YMCA and came home covered in red dirt and sweat. Most days, he and Cotton ended up in some kind of wrestling match, throwing sofa cushions at each other until Cotton ended up whining to Mrs. Odom.

Some days it was so hot, me and Howard would lay on the porch with ice cubes on our foreheads and tell knock-knock jokes. One day, Mr. Odom put a tarp in the bed of his pickup truck and filled it with water. We sat in there with our shorts and T-shirts on and ate frozen Kool-Aid in paper cups.

"I wish we could go to a real swimming pool," Howard said.

"When I go back to Raleigh," I said, "I'm gonna take swimming lessons like I did last summer."

"When are you going back to Raleigh?"

I shrugged. "I don't know for sure. I'm just saying . . . when I do . . ."

"Maybe if you stay in Colby, Daddy will drive us over to the lake one day," Howard said. "We can take Wishbone. I bet he'd like to swim."

"Maybe."

"Let's go down to the creek," Howard said.

I sighed. He'd been trying to get me to go back down to the creek behind his house for days, but I was nervous.

"What if Wishbone runs off again?" I said.

"Hold on to the leash real good," Howard said. "But really, Charlie, he don't wanna run off. He just made a mistake last time." He tossed a saltine cracker on the floor for Wishbone. "He came back, didn't he?"

So I finally said yes, and the three of us trudged down the path to the creek, with ferns tickling our legs and Wishbone sniffing at every little thing along the way. But when we got there, a bad, heavy feeling settled over me.

Instead of seeing the tiny silver minnows darting around the mossy rocks, I saw the look on Howard's face when I had said, "You wished you didn't have that up-down walk." And even though he acted like he didn't care anymore, for me those words still hovered in the air between us like a storm cloud.

I tossed a pebble into the creek and watched the water ripple and the minnows scatter. "I'm sorry for what I said, Howard."

When he looked a little puzzled, I added, "About you wishing you didn't have that up-down walk."

"Oh." He tossed a pebble into the creek, too, and Wishbone leaped in after it, sending up a spray of cold water.

"I know that was a mean thing to say and I'm sorry," I said.

I waited for Howard to say, "That's okay," but he didn't.

I waited for him to say, "Don't worry about it," but he didn't.

I waited for him to say, "Aw, heck, Charlie, I forgot all about that," but he didn't.

In fact, he didn't say anything for the longest time, and then he shrugged and said, "I'm used to kids saying mean things about the way I walk."

Ouch!

Stab me in the heart, Howard!

Toss me into the Mean Pile with all the other hateful kids in Colby.

Squish me into the mud like the worm that I am.

My eyes darted from tree to rock to creek to fern while I scrambled to figure out what to say next. And then I spied it. A blackbird feather nestled in the leaves and pine needles beside the creek.

"Look!" I said, grabbing the feather and holding it up for Howard to see.

He squinted at it, pushing his glasses further up on his freckled nose.

"Something to wish on," I said. "You stick it in the ground and make a wish." I held it out to him. "Here. You take it. Make a wish."

He shook his head. "Naw."

"Why not?"

He took his glasses off and wiped drops of creek water off of them with the edge of his shirt. Then he put them back on and said, " 'Cause I know my wish ain't never coming true."

Well, now, *that* surprised me, coming from Howard, who was always Mr. Positive.

"How do you know that?" I asked.

"I just do."

"But look at *me*," I said. "I've made the same wish every day since fourth grade and it hasn't come true yet." I stroked the top of Wishbone's wet head. "But if I make that wish enough times, I know it will someday."

"Then I hope it does," Howard said.

I held the feather out to him again. "You sure?"

He nodded.

So I stuck the feather into the soft dirt beside the creek, closed my eyes, and made my wish.

On the way home that day, the feeling that had been weighing me down so much since I'd said that mean thing to Howard felt a little bit lighter. I wasn't sure if I had fixed my mistake, but at least I had tried.

Twenty

When Bertha told me Jackie was coming to visit, my thoughts bounced every which way. I was excited as all get-out to see her. I'd missed her like crazy and hoped she'd been missing me, too. But I had some of ole Scrappy's anger simmering inside me. It seemed like she was so busy being happy that she didn't have time to think about me.

The day we were going to pick her up at the bus station in Asheville, I spent the morning practicing tricks with Wishbone. I wanted Jackie to see how smart he was and how much he loved me. Then I tried to make my room look like a real bedroom and not like a place to store canning jars.

First, I pulled my bedspread way up so it covered my

Cinderella pillowcases. Then I tacked a towel over the shelves to hide those jars. I put Wishbone's toys in a shoebox and wrote his name on the side with a marker while he sat there watching me with his head cocked. Every now and then he took out a tennis ball or a dirty rubber bone but I put it back.

"We want everything to look nice for Jackie," I told him.

Next, I pushed Gus's old jackets and sweaters to the back of the closet and hung up some of my T-shirts so it looked like I had a whole closet of my own. Then I put a towel over Bertha's sewing machine and hung my backpack on the hook on the closet door.

When I was done, I stood in the doorway and glanced around. It looked better, but I knew it wasn't anything like the room Jackie shared with Carol Lee. I bet they had matching floral bedspreads with heart-shaped throw pillows and pictures of rock stars taped on their headboards. I'm sure they had a dresser with a tray of nail polish and a jewelry box full of bracelets. They probably had pink-and-gold diaries with little keys and bags of potato chips under their beds to share at night while they talked about how happy they were. And I was sure they didn't have a single canning jar in their room. Not one.

On the ride to Asheville, Bertha pointed out some of the things she hadn't showed me before when we went to the mall.

"That place there has the best boiled peanuts in North Carolina."

"The Blue Ridge Parkway is up yonder."

"That road there goes to Blowing Rock, where the Tweetsie Railroad is."

I said "Oh" and "Yeah" and "Uh-huh," but really I was thinking about Jackie. Maybe I shouldn't have fixed up my room so much. Maybe if I'd left it the way it was, she'd feel sorry for me and take me back to Raleigh with her.

"Aw, Charlie," she'd say. "You can't stay here in this little ole room sleeping on a baby Cinderella pillow." She'd toss her hair over her shoulder and add, "This house is liable to fall right off the mountain if you sneeze too hard. You'd better come on back home with me."

While Bertha told me about the Mile High Swinging Bridge on Grandfather Mountain, I thought about me and Wishbone at Carol Lee's house. But then I started to worry. What if Carol Lee's parents didn't like dogs? What if they didn't like *me*?

Before I had time to stack up too many worries, we pulled into the bus station.

When we got out of the car, Bertha gave my shoulder a jiggle and said, "Are you excited?"

"Sort of," I said, but the truth was my insides were swirling like crazy.

We sat in a row of sticky vinyl seats and waited for Jackie's bus to get there. Bertha chatted with some woman who had a bunch of wild kids running around the bus station. Once, they tipped over the newspaper stand and she didn't even say anything. Gus fell asleep after about a minute, his head nodding until his chin dropped down onto his chest and his cheeks puffing out with every breath. I sure hoped he didn't call me Butterbean in front of Jackie.

Finally the man behind the ticket counter called out, "Bus number 94 arriving from Raleigh!"

And before I knew it, Jackie was swooping toward me, tall and tan and smiling. I could practically see the happiness floating above her like a halo.

The first thing she did was turn her head sideways, point to the bright blue streaks in her dark hair, and say, "Like it?"

"Um, it's okay," I said.

"Scrappy had a hissy fit." She grinned. "But you know what I say?" She tossed her head so her blue-streaked hair swished back over her shoulder. "I say, Who cares? 'Cause this is the new me."

The new me?

What did that mean?

Was that like a new life?

Maybe Jackie had gone and found herself a new life like Mama had tried to do all those years ago. A life that didn't include me.

On the ride back to Colby, Jackie and Bertha jabbered away like they'd been best friends forever. By the time we got home, they had every minute of every day planned out.

Bertha was gonna teach Jackie how to fry chicken and sew a zipper in a skirt.

They were gonna visit the thrift shop over in Fairview to look for a football jersey Jackie needed for a play she was in at Carol Lee's church.

They were gonna pick squash in the garden for Jackie to take back to Raleigh, and Bertha was gonna share her super-secret recipe for squash casserole with cream of mushroom soup.

On and on.

Jabber, jabber.

Hello? I thought. What about me? Anybody wanna do something with *me*?

Bertha must've read my mind or noticed my slumping shoulders, 'cause when we got out of the car, she said, "And I bet Charlie's dying to show you around Colby. She knows every nook and cranny now." She winked at me. "Right, Charlie?"

"I guess."

"And just *wait* until you see Wishbone!" Bertha said.

As soon as we got inside, Wishbone came leaping toward us, ears flapping and tail wagging. I knelt down and let him lick my face.

"Eww," Jackie said. "Don't let a dog tongue get in your mouth."

"He's just kissing me." I pressed my cheek against his nose. "He loves me."

Jackie made a face.

"And watch this," I said. I showed her how Wishbone could sit and shake and roll over.

"Wow, Charlie," Jackie said. "I never knew you were such a good dog trainer."

"Well, he's pretty easy to train 'cause he's so smart. And by the time we get back to Raleigh, I bet he'll know a whole lot more stuff."

Jackie lifted her eyebrows and squeezed her lips

together, but she didn't say anything. She strolled around the tiny living room, studying photos of old people on the table beside the couch, peeking into Bertha's yarn basket, peering into the kitchen.

"I love your house," she said to Bertha.

"Gus's grandaddy built it with his own two hands," Bertha said. "Ain't that right, Gus?"

Gus blushed a little and nodded.

"Check out the back porch," Bertha said, motioning toward the kitchen.

The next thing I knew, Jackie was out there raving about the view and the mountains and all. I sat on the floor in the living room with Wishbone snuggled in my lap, listening to this new Jackie and wondering what had happened to the old Jackie. The one who went to my dance recital while Mama and Scrappy stayed home and yelled at each other. The one who spent her allowance to buy me one of those friendship bracelets the other girls at school had. The one who made cupcakes for me to take to school on my birthday while Mama watched soap operas in her bathrobe.

That Jackie was gone and in her place was this new Jackie with blue streaks in her hair, out on the porch telling Bertha how much she loved the Blue Ridge

Mountains. And then this new Jackie went and said something the old Jackie never would have said:

"Charlie is *so* lucky to be here with y'all."

Lucky? She thinks I'm lucky I got yanked out of the only place I'd ever known my whole life and sent off to live with people I'd never laid eyes on before? Lucky my family was all broken up and scattered every which way?

Then Bertha said, "No, me and Gus are the lucky ones, right, Gus?"

"Right," Gus said.

When they came back in from the porch, Bertha said, "Charlie, why don't you take Jackie back to your room so she can put her things away."

I led Jackie to that tiny room and waited for her to say what I'd been imagining she'd say, like how awful it was. Even though I'd fixed it up, she'd say it was way too small. She'd peek behind that tacked-up towel and see those canning jars and then she'd say I'd better go back to Raleigh with her.

But no. This new Jackie said, "I *love* this room, Charlie. Can you believe you've got a room all to yourself and don't have to share anymore like we did back home?"

Well, didn't that beat all? "I liked sharing a room back home," I said, making my voice sound pitiful.

I was going to show her Gus's clothes jammed in my closet, but she flopped onto the bed and said, "Well, yeah, but it's nice to have a room that's just yours. Nobody leaving their dirty socks on the floor or taking up all the space on the dresser." She kicked her sandals off and leaned against the wall. "Don't get me wrong. I like Carol Lee and all. But sometimes I wish I could be by myself. Not have her snooping through my stuff or using my makeup without even asking."

She tossed her hair over her shoulder and said, "I just love Gus and Bertha, don't you?"

Now I have to say, that question caught me off guard, and I surprised myself when I didn't hesitate one little bit and said, "I do."

Did I love Gus and Bertha? I hadn't ever really thought about it before, but maybe I did. But then, everybody loves Gus and Bertha 'cause that's the kind of people they are.

"And you got yourself a dog, Charlie!" she said, rubbing her bare foot along Wishbone's back. "It seems like everything's turned out so good for you. Your very own room and your very own dog. Living with two nice people who don't cuss and holler at each other every minute of the day."

Then she jumped up off the bed and said, "Show me the garden."

That night, Bertha made grilled cheese sandwiches and potato salad for supper, and then we sat out on the porch under the orange sky streaked with gray-blue clouds. The smell of rain mingled with the sweet scent of honeysuckle, and crickets chirped in the huckleberry bushes along the edge of the woods.

Bertha and Jackie talked about boys, and if I didn't know better, it would've been hard to tell which one of them was a teenager and which one was a grown-up woman. Bertha told Jackie about the first time she ever met Gus when he fixed a flat tire on her daddy's car out on Highway 14.

"I'd never laid eyes on such a handsome boy in my life," she said. "My friend Jayme flirted her head off with him, but I knew I was the one he had eyes for. Right, Gus?" She poked Gus, and he nodded while he chewed on a toothpick.

Later, me and Jackie went back to my room and played Crazy Eights while she told me about some boy she'd been dating named Scooter. He was the paintball champion of Wake County and had a cousin in the Marines he wanted to fix up with Carol Lee.

Jackie had brought nail polish with her, so we painted our fingernails and told the same jokes we'd told about a million times before.

"What do you call a cow that eats your grass?" Jackie said.

"A lawn moo-er," I said. "What do frogs order in restaurants?"

"French flies."

We laughed like those were the funniest jokes in the world. For the first time since she'd showed me her blue-streaked hair at the bus station, she seemed like the old Jackie, and I realized how much I'd been missing her.

After we turned out the lights, she fell asleep in no time flat. Her soft snoring drifted through the air, reminding me of all those nights we'd shared in our room back home. I thought about how we laid there in the dark and listened to Mama and Scrappy fussing and fighting. When I was little, sometimes I'd crawl in bed with Jackie and she would sing right in my ear so I couldn't hear the mean words they hurled at each other.

Now here we were sleeping in the same room together again, Jackie in my bed and me in a sleeping bag on the floor with Wishbone. Except this time, the only sounds I heard were Jackie's soft snoring and the bullfrogs down in the woods. And then I thought about Jackie raving about this house and that porch and my very own room. In my head, I could still hear her saying how she just loved Gus and Bertha and telling me how everything's turned out so good for me. But then I thought, what's so good about being tossed out of my own house and riding the bus with those giggling kids and feeling for all the world like a stray dog with no place to call home? I hugged Wishbone closer and kissed his nose, while my thoughts bounced around so much they finally wore me out and I fell asleep.

Twenty-One

I spent the next few days watching Jackie flit around Colby like she'd lived there her whole life. She talked about high school football with the mailman and took cold fried chicken to Bertha's knitting club. She set up a vegetable stand at the end of the driveway and chatted with everybody who stopped to buy beans and squash, telling them about Raleigh and her waitress job and her new driver's license. And at the thrift shop in Fairview, as I watched her laughing with the owner about a big ugly hat somebody brought in, I felt like I was seeing her for the first time. Maybe this *was* the new Jackie. How come I had never noticed how much everybody loved her? Even Bertha's cats couldn't get enough of her, rubbing their heads against her legs and purring in her lap.

Every one of the Odom boys was red-faced and tongue-tied around her, falling all over each other to open the car door for her or bring her cold lemonade every time we went over there.

"I can't believe you know how to rebuild an engine," she said to Burl the first day we visited. And the next thing you know, she's out there in the driveway squinting down at a carburetor or something like it was the most fascinating thing she'd ever seen. Every now and then, she flipped her hair over her shoulder and I thought Burl was going to melt into a puddle right there in the gravel driveway.

Mrs. Odom brought powdered sugar doughnuts out on the porch and we sat around and listened to Jackie tell Waffle House stories.

"And *one* time," she said, "this old lady came in a limo driven by a chauffeur." She brushed powdered sugar off her lap. "Can you imagine going to the Waffle House in a chauffeur-driven limo?"

Everybody agreed they couldn't imagine that.

"But she left me a twenty-dollar tip for a four-dollar waffle, so I'm not complaining," Jackie said.

Howard and Dwight bugged their eyes out and said, "Wow!"

She told us how she and the other waitresses called it the Awful House, and those boys all hooted and hollered like that was the funniest thing they'd ever heard.

Then she told everybody about Raleigh. How big it is and all the malls and tanning salons and even an indoor miniature golf course.

"Y'all should come visit some time," she said. "I have my driver's license and Carol Lee has a car."

They grinned and nodded and said how much they'd like to go to Raleigh, and I felt jealousy poking at me so hard it made me squirm as I sat there on the porch steps.

Late that afternoon, me and Howard took Jackie down to the creek with Wishbone, and she didn't waste a minute taking her shoes off and wading into the cold mountain water, her laughter echoing through the trees. She answered all Howard's nosy questions without a single eye roll and acted like she hung out with up-down boys every day of her life.

"What's it like when you visit your daddy in jail?" he said.

I like to died when he asked that, but Jackie wasn't one bit bothered.

"Not as cool as it looks on TV, I can tell you that," she said. "We just sit at a table and talk about school and stuff. He tells me how bad the food is there and how the first thing he's gonna do when he gets out is eat about fourteen hamburgers."

I wanted to ask her if they ever talked about me, but I was scared the answer would be no and I would look like a loser in front of Howard.

I started to remind him that Scrappy is in a correctional facility, not a jail, but he and Jackie had already moved on to talking about that Bible Detective game at Sunday school.

"I bet Charlie's terrible at that game," she said, giving me a poke. "Reading the Bible was not exactly a popular activity at our house, right, Charlie?" She poked me again.

That night, Mrs. Odom invited me and Jackie to have supper with them. Burl and Lenny brought aluminum lawn chairs in from the yard for us and nearly knocked each other over trying to sit next to Jackie. She helped Mrs. Odom put plates of ham and bowls of cole slaw and baked beans on the table and didn't even blink an eye when everyone held hands and Dwight said the blessing and thanked the Lord for baked beans and new friends.

I swear, I felt invisible while everybody jibber-jabbered

at that table. Jackie told them about being a majorette in tenth grade and marching in the Memorial Day parade in the rain.

"Talk about a bad hair day!" she said, and everyone laughed. Then she asked Mr. Odom about his job driving a lumber truck. When he described driving from Colby to Charlotte to Greenville and everywhere in between, she said, "It must be so fun to go to all those different places." Then she went on to tell him about her friend Loretta, who worked the night shift at a truck stop on the interstate and, boy, oh, boy, did she have some stories to tell about some of those truckers.

Mr. Odom blushed a little at that, and Mrs. Odom jumped in real quick to tell us about Howard being the Bible Detective champion at church.

"No way!" Jackie said. "He didn't tell me that!" And then it was Howard's turn to blush.

Wishbone laid on the floor next to Cotton 'cause he knew there would be food down there before long. Sure enough, he gobbled up a couple of pieces of ham and some cornbread crumbs, and Jackie said, "Wishbone! Stop that!"

But Mrs. Odom said, "That's okay. Shoot, helps me keep the floor clean."

Jackie laughed her sparkly laugh, and in that very minute I wanted to be her. I wanted her easy way of making people love her. I wanted her knack for seeing the good in things. I even wanted her shiny black hair with blue streaks. But no matter how bad I wanted it, I was still going to be just plain old me.

Twenty-Two

That Sunday, we piled into Gus's car and headed down the mountain to church. Jackie had french braided my hair like she used to back in Raleigh, and Bertha made a fuss over it.

"I just *love* Charlie's hair like that!" she said. "Jackie, you should get a job in a beauty parlor. You have real talent."

Jackie thwacked her forehead and said she couldn't believe she'd never thought of that before. "I might look into that when I get home," she said.

So then Bertha told us a story about her friend Denise who flunked out of beauty school.

"Just flunked right out after three weeks and ended up marrying some rich guy. But not two months later, she ran off to Atlanta with that rich guy's brother."

Jackie loved Bertha's stories and always laughed or said "No way" or "I can't believe that" while me and Gus just sat in silence, pretending to be interested.

After church, Jackie snatched cookies off the food table in the fellowship hall and then went to hang out with the teenagers in the parking lot like she'd known them her whole life. How had Jackie and I turned out so different? I was sure she never worried one little bit whether or not anybody liked her. But then, of course, everybody *did* like her, so what was there to worry about?

That afternoon, the Odoms came over to Gus and Bertha's for dinner. Bertha always made a big deal out of Sunday dinner, but with the Odoms coming it was a regular feast.

Jackie and I helped her set up some card tables out in the yard. We pushed them together and then put a sheet over them for a tablecloth, and Jackie set out mason jars filled with wildflowers.

"Looks like the Queen of England is coming for dinner," Gus said.

Bertha bustled around the kitchen, and before long the house was filled with all kinds of good smells and the countertops were covered with bowls of black-eyed peas and turnip greens. Squash casseroles and sliced tomatoes. Fried okra and succotash. Biscuits and gravy. Brownies and peach cobbler. Then she took a big roast chicken out of the oven and said, "There! Now if I can keep the cats out of here, we're all set."

Of course, Wishbone sat by the kitchen door with his nose twitching in the air and his tail wagging a mile a minute.

"Not yet, boy," I told him. "Maybe later."

Then we heard Burl's truck on the gravel driveway, and me and Wishbone ran out to greet the Odoms.

All those redheaded boys spilled out of the back of the truck, and the front yard that was usually so quiet except for the birds on the fence post or the sputter of the sprinkler in the garden turned into a flurry of commotion. Dwight and Lenny running and punching and climbing on the fence. Cotton chasing after the cats. Mrs. Odom hurrying inside to help Bertha with the food. Mr. Odom and Gus out in the lawn chairs talking about the NASCAR race over in Charlotte last week. Howard and me tossing a tennis ball for Wishbone to catch.

Then Jackie came outside looking like Miss America, and I thought Burl was going to faint right there in the red dirt. Everybody else had changed out of their church clothes except Jackie. When she came strutting across the yard in her white sundress and bare feet, I don't think I'd ever seen her look so pretty. I still had that french braid in my hair, so maybe I looked pretty, too, even in my shorts and ratty T-shirt. I hoped so. But I knew I could never look as pretty as Jackie.

Before long, Bertha told everybody to go inside and load up their plates, and those boys like to busted the door down racing to the kitchen. Then we sat at the card tables in the yard and held hands while Mr. Odom said the blessing. Gus and Bertha weren't the blessing type, but I guess they did it to be nice to their company. Mr. Odom sure had a lot of stuff to be thankful for, everything from this beautiful day to those turnip greens. Then he said, "And thank you for sending these two fine young ladies to shine their light on us here in Colby."

I knew I was supposed to have my eyes closed, but I took a peek and there was Jackie grinning and winking at me.

As soon as we all said a loud "Amen," everybody dove into their food like there was no tomorrow. Mrs. Odom and Bertha kept running back into the kitchen to bring out more tomatoes or succotash while Jackie poured sweet tea and Gus shooed cats away. Wishbone sat by Cotton hoping he'd drop a chicken leg.

By the time Bertha brought out dessert, everybody was rubbing their stomachs and saying how they couldn't possibly eat another bite, except, well, maybe just a little of that peach cobbler.

Cotton leaned across the table to grab a brownie and said, "Hey, look! The wishbone!"

Sure enough, right there on that greasy platter was the chicken wishbone.

Of course, my *dog*, Wishbone, heard his name and ran over to Cotton, probably thinking he was about to get something good to eat.

"Who wants to pull the wishbone with me?" Cotton said.

Dwight jumped up. "Me!" he said.

"No!" I hollered, pushing Dwight out of the way. "It has to be me!"

Cotton held the bone behind his back when Dwight tried to grab it.

"I called it first, Charlie," Dwight said.

I stamped my foot. "No! It's mine!" I could feel anger flooding over me and it was all I could do to keep myself from shoving Dwight.

Then Howard hurried over and whispered "Pineapple" in my ear just as I was stamping my foot again.

172

Jackie shook my shoulder and snapped, "Good grief, Charlie, quit making such a fuss over a silly ole bone."

But Howard piped up and said, "Come on, Dwight, let Charlie pull the wishbone."

Uh-oh. Was Howard going to tell everybody about me making a wish every day? I hadn't told him not to tell anybody and now I bet he was and everybody was going to think I was crazy.

But he didn't.

He told Dwight he'd give him some of his Bible bucks if he'd let me pull the wishbone with Cotton.

"How many?" Dwight asked.

"Three."

"Make it five."

"Okay."

So Dwight ran off to grab another brownie and Cotton held the wishbone out to me. We each took a side and closed our eyes. I made my wish and then I pulled.

Snap!

That bone broke in two and guess what? I got the big side! The side that's supposed to make your wish come true.

"Dang it!" Cotton said, tossing his piece of the bone onto the table.

Before I had a chance to thank Howard for helping me like that, Mr. Odom announced that it was time for them to go, and they piled back into Burl's truck.

I knew I should've joined Jackie and helped Bertha clean up in the kitchen, but instead, I sat out in the yard with my arm around Wishbone and watched that truck bounce up the gravel driveway, loaded with all those good-hearted Odoms. When they turned onto the road, I hollered, "Thank you!" I figured Howard probably wouldn't hear me, but then I saw him give me a thumbs-up before the truck disappeared from sight.

Twenty-Three

On Jackie's last day in Colby, she and Bertha sat together at the sewing machine in my room and talked about boys and clothes and movie stars while they worked on a zipper. I took Wishbone out in the yard and pulled weeds from between the marigolds beside the garden shed while he slept in the sun.

I hated thinking about Jackie getting on that bus to Raleigh, going back to her happy life, painting her fingernails with Carol Lee, dating Scooter the paintball champion, maybe even going to beauty school. Each yank of a weed was like a jab in my heart as I thought about her leaving me behind. By the time Jackie and Bertha finished that zipper, there wasn't a single weed left in that yard and my heart ached so bad I wanted to cry.

Later that day, me and Jackie and Wishbone went

down to the Odoms' so Jackie could say goodbye. The boys sat on the porch steps looking like they were going to a funeral.

"Y'all better come visit me in Raleigh," Jackie said. She threw her arms out wide. "Everybody. We'll have us the best time ever."

They nodded solemnly and Cotton swiped at tears.

"If I'm still working at that ole Waffle House, y'all come by and I'll throw in a couple of chocolate chip waffles for free."

Cotton perked up. "Chocolate chip waffles?"

Jackie nodded. "Yep. And I'll make sure they put extra chips in yours, okay?"

He grinned.

"I bet Charlie's gonna miss you," Howard said.

Jackie put her arm around my shoulder. "Well, I'm gonna miss her, too. But she can come visit."

"Visit?" I said. "I'll be going back there to *live*." I rubbed my hand down Wishbone's back. "You know, when Mama gets her feet on the ground," I added.

Jackie looked down at her lap. Wishbone's tail swished back and forth in the dry red dirt.

"Well, then," Jackie said. "I reckon it's time for me to get my hugs in." She held her arms out.

Each of those boys gave her a quick, awkward hug.

Then Mrs. Odom ran out of the house and said, "It was just a joy and a blessing having you here in Colby, Jackie."

Then she and Jackie hugged, and we headed back home.

That night, Bertha made a special supper of meat loaf and lima beans, fried green tomatoes, and sweet potato pie. Wishbone laid beside my chair waiting for somebody to toss him a piece of meat loaf every now and then. I have to admit that we'd spoiled him rotten and turned him into a world-class beggar.

After we sat out on the porch for a while, me and Jackie went back to my room. I brushed Wishbone while Jackie packed, stuffing her shorts and things into her duffel bag and telling me again how lucky I was to have such a nice place to live.

I watched her gather her nail polish and toss it into the duffel bag, and I started to feel more pitiful by the minute.

"What's going to happen to me?" I wanted to ask her. But I didn't.

After we turned the lights out, I stared up at the ceiling, watching the shadows of the dogwood tree dance in the moonlight. Then I took a deep breath and said, "Can I go back to Raleigh with you?"

The silence that followed nearly swallowed me up. I could feel my heart beat in my chest and Wishbone's warm breath against my cheek. Then Jackie got out of bed and sat beside my sleeping bag.

"Nothing's gonna change, Charlie," she said. "I used to think it would but now I don't. Scrappy is gonna keep being Scrappy and Mama is gonna keep being Mama and you and I are on our own. No magic wand is gonna fix things."

I didn't want to believe that, so I pushed those words away so I wouldn't have to think about them. Then I said, "Did you know Mama left us when we were little? Just ran off with a garbage bag full of clothes to start a new life?"

Jackie heaved a big sigh. "Yes, I did know that."

"How'd you know?"

"When you're seven years old and your mama waltzes out the door without so much as a goodbye, well, that's something you don't forget."

"How come you never told me?" I said.

She put her hand on my back and rubbed in little circles. "'Cause I didn't want you to hate Mama," she said.

"Do *you* hate Mama?"

"Naw." She pushed my hair behind my ear. "I don't like her very much, but I don't hate her."

"But why can't I live with you?" I asked so quiet it was almost a whisper.

Jackie hugged her knees. "Charlie, I can't live with Carol Lee forever. I'm saving my money and me and Wylene Jarvis are getting an apartment together. I can't take care of you like Gus and Bertha can," she said. "Shoot, I can barely take care of myself."

We sat in silence for a minute. Then Jackie said, "You got a good life here, Charlie. You got Gus and Bertha loving you and treating you like a princess. You got all those Odoms thanking the good Lord for you. Then there's Howard, the nicest friend you could ever want. You got these beautiful mountains and a garden and a porch to sit on that's like sitting on the side of heaven."

Wishbone kicked his legs and let out a little woof like he was having a doggie dream. Jackie rubbed his stomach. "And a dog that loves you like nobody's business."

I looked at Wishbone and thought about Bertha saying how dogs love you no matter what, and my heart nearly burst.

"Don't hate me, Charlie," Jackie said.

Hate her?

I loved everything about her. I loved the old Jackie *and* the new Jackie. Why couldn't I tell her that? I guess I hadn't had much practice saying "I love you." So I just sat there in the darkness with Wishbone twitching in his sleep beside me and said, "I do like those blue streaks in your hair."

Twenty–Four

The week after Jackie left, I started Vacation Bible School at Rocky Creek Baptist Church. I'd told Bertha I didn't want to go but she kept telling me how much I was gonna love it.

"I went to Vacation Bible School every summer when I was a girl," she said. "I loved everything about it. The games. The crafts. The songs."

She went on to tell me about making a bird feeder by putting peanut butter on a pine cone and rolling it in bird seed. "And lanyards? I must've made about a hundred lanyards." She laughed and shook her head. "And macrame keychains. I loved those. *And*," she said, "Howard and all the kids from Sunday school will be there."

So I finally said okay, but then the day before I was

supposed to go, Bertha came home with a lunch box covered with ponies and rainbows.

"I can't believe I let you take your lunch to school in an ugly ole paper bag," she said.

"I can't take *that*!" I said.

Bertha's smile faded. "Oh," she said. "Okay."

I could tell I'd hurt her feelings, but there was no way I could take that lunch box.

Bertha snatched it off the kitchen counter and stuck it way up on the top shelf of the cupboard. "I don't know what I was thinking," she said. "That thing is just plum silly."

So she put my lunch in a brown paper bag and off I went to Vacation Bible School.

We sat in a circle in the shade and listened to Miss Rhonda tell us how much fun we were going to have. Even though we knew each other from Sunday school, she said, "First, I'd like for each of y'all to tell us your name and then three fun facts about yourself."

Right away, I thought about my first day of school in Colby and that "Getting to Know You" paper. But this time, when it was my turn, instead of saying I liked soccer, ballet, and fighting, I said, "I have a dog named Wishbone. My sister works at the Waffle House. My aunt Bertha has seven cats."

We spent the morning making papier-mâché bowls and singing a song about Moses in the bulrushes. When it was time for lunch, I got my brown paper bag and sat next to Audrey Mitchell. I'd made up my mind I was going to be more like Jackie from now on. Cool and confident, making friends right and left.

But before I could think up something to say to Audrey, Howard plopped down next to me.

"Burl wrote Jackie a letter," he said.

"What for?"

He shrugged. "Lenny snatched it right out of his hand and they got in a fight. Burl chased him around the house cussing and broke a lamp." He lifted the corner of his sandwich and examined the bologna and mustard inside.

"Did Burl get the letter back?" I asked.

Howard flattened his sandwich between the palms of his hands. "Yeah," he said, "but it got ripped, and now they're both grounded 'cause of the cussing and the lamp." He pushed at his damp red hair. His arms were sunburned bright pink and dotted with freckles. He went on to tell me about Dwight breaking his pinkie finger at baseball camp.

While Howard talked, I watched Audrey out of the corner of my eye. She sat cross-legged with a paper napkin on her lap. She had butterfly barrettes in her hair, and her sneakers didn't have one speck of dirt on them. Her lunch box was plain. No ponies or rainbows on it. She opened it and peered inside. Then she took out a plastic bag full of grapes, something wrapped in foil, and a folded-up piece of paper.

I scooted a little closer to her and pretended like I was listening to Howard while she opened the paper. It was a note with big swirly handwriting. When she put it down on the grass next to her grapes, I squinted at it, trying to read it.

"And Cotton had two ticks on him," Howard was saying. "So Mama made him strip down naked right there in the yard."

A couple of kids giggled and I shot Howard a look. Nobody wanted to hear the word *naked* while they ate their lunch. But Howard went right on talking like he didn't even notice.

Just then some girl I didn't know said, "Sit here, Audrey," and patted the ground next to her. So Audrey scooped up her grapes and stuff and moved away from me and Howard, leaving that piece of paper behind. Right away, I slapped my foot down on top of it.

While Audrey and that girl chatted away about swimming lessons and soccer camp, I snatched up the paper and stuffed it in my pocket.

"What was that?" Howard asked.

"What was what?"

"That paper."

"What paper?"

"That paper in your pocket."

"Nothing."

Howard wiped at a dab of mustard on his shorts. "Okay," he said.

All afternoon, while we read Bible stories out loud and watched Miss Rhonda's teenage son do magic tricks, I thought about that note in my pocket. Every once in a while, I reached in and wrapped my fingers around it.

Finally I got my chance. Howard was helping Miss Rhonda take the Bible storybooks back inside the church, and Audrey was busy being friends with everybody but me. So I took that paper out of my pocket and read it.

Have fun at Vacation Bible School. I will be missing you. I love you very much.

Mama

Quickly I folded it and jammed it back into my pocket. I looked over at Audrey linking arms with some girl and whispering. I closed my eyes, and in my mind, I became Audrey. A girl with perfect sneakers and a friend to whisper secrets to and a mama who wrote "I love you very much" on a note for me. But then I opened my eyes and I was me again.

That night we had corn on the cob for supper. I counted the rows of corn on my cob and I couldn't believe it. Exactly fourteen. That was on my list of things you can wish on. I counted one more time to make sure and then I closed my eyes and made my wish.

"Oh, I almost forgot!" Bertha said, jumping up from the table. She took something off the counter and handed it to me.

A lunch box.

A plain lunch box with no ponies or rainbows.

She lifted her eyebrows and said, "What do you think? Better?"

A wave of guilt swept over me and caught me by surprise. I felt bad that Bertha had spent money to buy another lunch box for me. I should've just taken the one with rainbows and ponies and been thankful for it. I bet Jackie would have. But I hadn't, and now here was Bertha being so nice to me.

"Yes, ma'am," I said. "Thank you."

Then we went out on the porch and tossed a tennis ball to Wishbone till he got tired and went to sleep at my feet. As I watched the sun sink slowly behind the mountains, I cupped my hand around that note in my pocket. I thought about Audrey's mother putting those grapes in that little bag and writing that note. I wondered what Audrey's family was like. The one she had written on her flower for the Garden of Blessings at church. I knew for sure her daddy wasn't away somewhere getting corrected. And I bet she had a sister who played cards with her on rainy days and whispered secrets under the covers at night. And I was certain her mama had her feet on the ground.

When it got dark and the mosquitoes came out, me and Wishbone went back to my room. I fished around in my backpack until I found a piece of paper and a pen. I tore the paper in half and sat on the floor and wrote:

I love you very much. Mama

Then I folded the paper up and tucked it under my pillow before turning out the light and kissing Wishbone on the top of his head.

Twenty-Five

The next day at Bible school, we made bottle-cap magnets with the Ten Commandments on them. Then we played some game where we had to wrap ourselves in strips of crepe paper like Joseph's coat of many colors and race around an obstacle course. I guess Miss Rhonda didn't remember about Howard and his up-down walk when she thought up that game. He came in last and ripped his coat of many colors, but he didn't seem to care.

At lunch, we sat in the shade and took out our lunch boxes. Howard was helping Miss Rhonda gather up all the crepe paper strips, so I plopped myself down next to Audrey.

"Hey," I said.

"Hey," Audrey said, and then she scooted closer to a girl named Lainie who had scabs all over her legs. I couldn't believe she'd rather sit closer to a scabby-legged girl than me, but I guess she did. I'd told her I was sorry about that kicking and shoving, hadn't I? I didn't know what else I could do to make friends with her.

I opened my new lunch box and took out the things that Bertha had packed for me. A bagel with peanut butter. Strawberries in a margarine tub. Some cookies she made that were kind of burnt on the bottom. Then I took out the note that I had written the night before. The one that said "I love you very much. Mama."

I opened it and held it out in front of me. Then I cleared my throat so maybe Audrey would look my way and see that paper, but she was busy stirring her yogurt.

So I tossed the paper on the grass almost in front of her.

"You dropped your trash," she said.

"What?"

"That's your trash." She pointed to the paper.

"You mean that note?"

She shrugged. "Whatever."

"It's from my mama," I said, rolling my eyes. "She's all the time doing that." I nudged the paper a little closer to her so maybe she would read it.

"I thought you lived with your aunt and uncle," she said.

"Well, not *all* the time. I mean, most of the time. But my mama comes to visit a lot and she's always writing these notes." I knew my face was beet red, so I kept my eyes on the ground.

Audrey made a face. "You're not supposed to lie at Vacation *Bible* School." She said the word *Bible* real loud and mean-sounding.

Before I knew it, I was standing over her with my fists balled up and my heart beating like crazy. I felt red-hot anger settle over me like a blanket. I wanted to stomp on her perfect sneakers. I wanted to yank those butterfly barrettes out of her hair. But then Howard came up from behind me saying, "Pineapple! Pineapple! Pineapple!"

Audrey grabbed her yogurt and lunch box and stood up. "Y'all are crazy," she said, and stormed off toward the church.

"What the heck, Charlie?" Howard said. "You gonna smack somebody at *church*?"

I dropped back down to the grass and began throwing my bagel and stuff into my lunch box.

Howard sat beside me. "Why're you so mad?"

"She said I lied."

"Did you?"

"No." I snatched that stupid note up and tossed it into the lunch box.

He looked at me over the top of his glasses the way some old grownup would. "Then no reason to get mad." He peered into my lunch box. "Are you gonna eat that bagel?"

It took me a while to simmer down, but I finally did. Still, I sure wasn't in the mood to memorize Bible verses. When it was almost time to go home, Miss Rhonda told us to go inside and help set up the chairs for Sunday school.

As Howard made his way toward the church, T. J. Rainey followed behind him, walking in an up-down way like Howard. He looked around to make sure everybody was watching, a big ole grin on his face like he was the funniest person in the universe.

Suddenly, Howard turned around, but T.J. didn't even stop. He kept walking toward Howard.

Up.

Down.

Up.

Down.

And then I couldn't believe my eyes. Howard just turned back around and went on his way like nothing had even happened.

Well, I can tell you for sure there weren't enough pineapples in the world to keep me from running straight at T.J., full steam ahead. I kept my arms stiff in front of me and bam! I shoved him so hard his head snapped back and he crashed face-first into the dirt.

I confess I was more than a little surprised when he got right up and shoved me back, knocking me to the ground. I scrambled to my feet and was ready to haul off and bust him one when Miss Rhonda stepped between me and T.J. with her fists jammed into her waist and a look of pure horror on her face.

"Stop it right now!" she hollered. "That is *not* Bible school behavior!"

So that's how I ended up sitting on a church pew with T. J. Rainey, listening to Miss Rhonda talk about forgiveness and kindness and goodness and grace and all that stuff. It seemed to me like Audrey Mitchell ought to be sitting here in her perfect sneakers while Miss Rhonda quoted some stuff about doing unto others. Every once in a while, T.J. shot me a glare and I shot one right back.

When Bertha came to pick me up, Miss Rhonda had to go and tell her what happened. Bertha nodded and said "Oh, dear," and "Yes, ma'am," and "I will," and then we rode home in silence. Mama would've been hollering at me, asking me what in the world was wrong with me and can't I go one dern day without causing trouble. But not Bertha. She reached over and patted my knee and said, "You are a good friend to Howard, Charlie."

When we got home, me and Wishbone went out front and sat in the shade of the dogwood tree. The air was still and hot. The red-dirt yard dry and dusty. Bertha's nasturtiums by the front door spilled over the sides of the flowerpots and drooped onto the ground. The sprinkler sputtered in circles out in the garden, leaving glistening drops of water dripping off the okra and settling into little pools inside the yellow flowers of the cucumber plants.

When I'd first gotten to Colby, most of that garden had been just rows of tiny green plants poking out of the ground. But now, plump red tomatoes grew fatter every day, yellow flowers turned into bright green zucchini, and pole beans hung in clusters from vines that snaked up twine to form leafy tepees.

A blue jay landed in the yard near us and Wishbone's

ears perked up. He cocked his head and watched that bird hop in and out of the marigolds along the fence. I put my arm around him and rubbed his long, velvety ears between my fingers. He licked my face, his tail swishing back and forth on the dusty ground.

"I swear that dog loves you to pieces," Bertha kept telling me.

And I do believe it was true. He'd gotten to where he wouldn't let me out of his sight, following me around from room to room, laying by my chair at the kitchen table, sleeping with his head on my feet out on the porch. I didn't even need to keep him on a leash out in the yard anymore. He stayed right by my side everywhere I went. He might trot over to sniff a shrub or snap at the bumblebees on the clover by the porch, but he always glanced back to make sure I was still there. And every time he did that, I loved him more.

After a while, Bertha came outside and brought us saltine crackers with peanut butter. She let Wishbone eat one right off of her hand and didn't even care when he slobbered on her. Then out of the clear blue she said, "Charlie, I really admire you for sticking up for Howard like you did today."

Admired me?

Well, that was a first.

I was pretty sure nobody on earth had ever admired me before.

"You do?" I said.

She nodded. "I do."

And so we sat out there in the shade of the dogwood while the sun beat down on the dirt yard. Bertha told me a story about when she and Mama were little girls and went to a lake one summer.

"Carla had never been in water deeper than a bathtub in her life," Bertha said. "So when she fell off the dock into that murky water, everybody went crazy. But, I swear, she popped right up like a cork without so much as a sputter. Then she just floated on her back staring up at the sky while everybody ran up and down the dock hollering and carrying on and my uncle Jarod jumped in after her and ruined his brand-new wristwatch." Bertha chuckled and swatted at gnats that were hovering over Wishbone as he slept. "That girl was a walking wonder sometimes," she said.

Of course, I couldn't help but ask myself how a woman who can't get out of bed and get her feet on the ground could be a walking wonder, but I was still basking in the glow of being admired. So, for once, I kept quiet and didn't mess things up.

"And one time," Bertha went on, "she snipped all the

buttons off my blouses." She cut the air with her fingers like scissors. "*Snip, snip, snip*. Right off onto the floor."

"Why'd she do that?"

"Beats the heck out of me," she said. "She did the craziest things you ever saw." She reached over suddenly and grabbed my knee. "Well, not *crazy* crazy, but just, you know, kind of, well, *odd*."

She let go of my knee and went back to swatting gnats away from Wishbone. "About the only thing I remember our poor mama ever saying was, 'Carla, stop that.'"

I nodded. I had a perfect picture in my mind of little Carla snipping those buttons. *Snip, snip, snip*.

Before long, Gus's car came bouncing and squeaking up the gravel driveway.

"Hey, Butterbean," he called out the window.

Then he got out, kissed Bertha on the cheek, patted Wishbone on the head, and told me I was a ray of sunshine at the end of a long, sorry day.

That night in bed, I laid on top of the cool sheets with Wishbone's soft, warm body next to me. I thought about my broken family back in Raleigh and wondered if they were thinking about me, a ray of sunshine at the end of a long, sorry day.

Twenty-Six

"What's that?"

Audrey Mitchell pointed to my hand as we played Bible bingo in the fellowship hall. It had been raining all morning, so we hadn't been able to go outside and have a balloon race like Miss Rhonda had planned for us to do.

I looked down at the drawing I had done on the back of my hand with a pen.

"A blackbird in a cage," I said, flipping my hair the way Jackie flips hers.

Audrey screwed up her face like she'd just seen a dead possum squashed flat in the middle of the road.

"Check it out," I said, thrusting my hand toward her face and winking. I'd been trying to do all the things

Jackie does. Flipping my hair and winking. Acting cool and confident. But so far, it didn't seem to be working. Most of those kids at Bible school still treated me like I had cooties.

"What's it for?" Audrey said.

And then the darnedest thing happened. I guess being a ray of sunshine had given me some *real* confidence, not *pretend* confidence, because I looked her square in the eye and said, "It's the same as the tattoo my daddy has on *his* hand."

The minute those confident words came out, old Mr. Doubt tapped me on the shoulder and said, "*Now* look what you've done. She's gonna ask you where your daddy is, and *then* what are you gonna say?"

But miracle of miracles, Audrey did *not* ask me where my daddy was. She just said, "Oh," and studied her Bible bingo card.

So I pushed Mr. Doubt aside and said, "His name is Scrappy, and he's getting corrected."

Audrey put another token on her bingo card. "What does that mean?" she asked.

"Means he's getting corrected," I said. "He'll be home any day now."

"So then are you going back to Raleigh?" she said.

At that, Howard's head shot up from studying his bingo card and he stared at me.

"Um, yeah," I said. "Sure."

"When?" Howard said.

I shrugged. "I don't know. However long it takes for Scrappy to get corrected, I guess."

Suddenly my confidence began to spin out of control. Faster and faster until it rose right up through the ceiling and out the roof of Rocky Creek Baptist Church, disappearing into the sky and leaving me there in the fellowship hall with a stomachache. I licked my thumb and wiped at that blackbird tattoo, leaving a smudgy black spot on my hand.

Suddenly somebody yelled, "Bingo!" and Miss Rhonda clapped her hands and pointed to the table full of prizes. Coloring books and glittery pens and erasers shaped like Noah's ark.

"Clear your cards," Miss Rhonda said. "Let's start a new game."

Later that day, me and Howard sat on the Odoms' front porch steps watching Wishbone and Cotton playing in the sprinkler. Cotton jumped over puddles of muddy water while Wishbone scampered along behind him, ears flopping and tail wagging.

"I been wondering about something," Howard said, scratching at mosquito bites on his freckled leg. "How come you shoved T.J. at Bible school yesterday?"

"What do you mean?" I asked.

"I mean, why'd you shove him?"

"He was making fun of you, Howard."

"I know."

I stared at him. His eyebrows were squeezed together over his glasses, and he looked so serious, for a minute I almost laughed. But then he said, "He was making fun of *me*, not *you*."

"Then you're the one who should've shoved him," I said.

"Naw."

"Why not?" I said. "Why do you let kids make fun of you and don't do one dern thing about it?"

"'Cause I'd be shoving somebody every day of my life."

"So?"

"So, what good is that?"

We sat in silence for a few minutes. Cotton was stomping in the mud and Wishbone was snapping at the water swirling out of the sprinkler.

"But why'd *you* shove T.J.?" Howard asked.

"Because he was being mean to you." I wiped muddy water off my legs. "Duh," I added.

"Why do you care about that?"

" 'Cause you're my friend," I said. "I don't like kids to be mean to my friends, okay?"

"I'm your friend?"

"Sure you are," I said. "Duh," I added again.

"I am?"

"Well, yeah."

"Then my wish came true!"

"It did?"

"Yeah." Howard blushed a little, his white freckly face turning pale pink. "Well, part of it anyway. I wished for two things. So, since one of 'em has come true, I can tell it to you. I wished that we'd be friends."

Well, dang! I never would've guessed that! You'd think that a redheaded boy with glasses who was named Howard and had an up-down walk would have a lot more to wish for than being friends with me. But I admit I felt a smile on my face and hope in my heart, 'cause maybe wishes really *do* come true. Maybe some wishes just take longer than others.

Twenty-Seven

The next day after Bible school, Wishbone and I were sitting out front while Gus worked in the garden. Tiny wrens and sparrows hopped around the yard and fluttered up to the bird feeder on the fencepost. After a while, Bertha came out with a couple of cats trailing along behind her. She smelled like lavender and I couldn't help but notice how much she looked like Mama, with her hair curling around her face and her eyes crinkled up at the edges.

I figured she was going to tell me a story about some lady in her knitting group or something, but she said, "I found that note."

My stomach squeezed up and I felt kind of scared for a minute.

"Um . . ."

"That note in your lunch box?" she said.

Well, what in the world could I say now? I felt like a big, dumb baby for writing that note. I wanted Bertha to go away. I did *not* want to talk about that note.

But Bertha did not go away. She sat petting the cat purring in her lap and gazing out at Gus weeding in the garden. And then she said, "You know, Charlie, me and Gus always wanted children." She rubbed Wishbone's belly with her bare foot. "We have had many blessings in our life together, but having children has not been one of them. So, um . . ."

I watched her foot rubbing Wishbone and waited.

"Well," she said. "I guess I'm just not too good at doing things that mothers do."

My heart sank and I scrambled to think of something to say, but I couldn't.

"When I saw that note I wanted to kick myself," she went on. "How come I didn't think how much a little girl would love a note like that in her lunch box? I wished like anything I had thought to do that but I didn't. Just like I didn't think how silly that rainbow lunch box was."

And then there was her hand on my knee. It was dark

and tan from hours in the sun. Fingernails rough and dirty from pulling weeds in the garden.

"So, I hope you'll be patient with me while I learn," she said.

I hung my head and nodded. I should've said something nice to her. I should've said, "Oh, don't even worry about it. That rainbow lunch box was no big deal." I should've said, "I don't even care about that dumb note."

But the truth was, all I could do was sit there feeling her warm hand and breathing her lavender smell.

"Let's go help Gus," she said.

So the three of us pulled weeds and picked beans and pinched dead flowers off the marigolds. Wishbone sat outside the gate and whined to get in, but he wasn't allowed because of his digging.

When we were done, we climbed into Gus's car and picked up Howard before heading down the mountain to get ice cream. Wishbone stuck his head out the window, his ears flapping like crazy in the wind, while me and Howard sang Bible school songs.

Every once in a while, we passed a clearing with a view of the mountains stretched out as far as you could see. A smoky blue haze floated over the treetops. It reminded me of my first day in Colby, when Gus had told me why these are called the Blue Ridge Mountains. Some-times it felt like just yesterday that I'd sat on the school bus with all those kids I didn't know, riding through this town and thinking every laundromat and trailer park and shabby little house along the way was the sorri-est thing I'd ever seen. But now here I was, singing Bible school songs with my friend Howard and my arms wrapped around my very own dog, and when I looked out at the now-familiar sights of Colby, I realized they didn't seem to look quite so sorry anymore.

Bertha chattered away in the front seat the whole way to town while Gus nodded silently. We got ice cream at the Dairy Freeze and sat at a picnic table trying to eat it quick before the summer heat made it run down our cones and drip onto our laps. Bertha scooped a little bit into a paper cup for Wishbone, and Howard let him have the last bite of his cone.

On the way home, me and Howard taught Gus and Bertha some of our Bible school songs, and then the best thing happened. I saw a yellow railroad car. That was on my list of things to wish on thanks to Fulton Banner, a crazy old man who lived next door to us in Raleigh.

"Yellow railroad cars aren't too plentiful," he told me. "When you see one, make a wish."

For a minute, I thought I might not even bother making my wish. Maybe I was just wasting my time. But then, something inside me told me not to give up and to keep on trying. I mean, you never know, right?

So I looked back at that yellow railroad car as we passed it and made my wish.

Twenty-Eight

And so the summer drifted by up there in the Blue Ridge Mountains. I was glad when Bible school was over and all I had to do was play cards on Howard's porch or take Wishbone down to the creek. Some days we rode our bikes to nowhere in particular, and once in a while we sold vegetables and bread-and-butter pickles out of a wagon at the end of our driveway. Mrs. Odom taught me how to crochet and helped me make a scarf for Bertha. Gus took me fishing and I even won a few Bible bucks in Sunday school.

Jackie called every now and then. She had a new boyfriend named Jake who drove a motorcycle. Carol Lee's parents didn't like him.

"But who cares?" she said. "Not me."

She didn't get the bank teller job she wanted, but she met some guy who needed a file clerk at his insurance agency, and then she could finally quit that Waffle House job.

I got a few more letters from Scrappy. He didn't say much except "It sure has been hot here lately" or "I'm getting fat eating jailhouse food. Ha ha."

I still made my wish every day because I decided I was not ready to give up yet. I wished on a butterfly that landed on me, on a camel-shaped cloud, on a cricket in the house, and a lightning bug glowing on my ring finger. I found another four-leaf clover and a penny in a parking lot, and one time we drove across the state line into Tennessee, which is good for wishing if you clap three times first.

And then one day a lady from social services showed up at Gus and Bertha's. She snooped around the house, her eyes flitting here and there, examining every little thing. She made a face at the cat hair on the couch and raised her eyebrows at those canning jars in my room. Bertha followed along behind her chattering a mile a minute about what a big help I am around the house and how much I'd loved Vacation Bible School. (Of course, she left out the parts about T. J. Rainey and that dumb lunch-box note.)

"And check out her dog!" she said, nodding toward Wishbone snoring by the back door. "You wouldn't believe how she takes care of that dog. Feeds him. Walks him. Lets him sleep right on her pillow every night."

That lady made another face and then asked if there was somewhere we could talk.

"Why don't we go out on the back porch?" Bertha said.

So we sat out on the porch with the afternoon sun high above the mountains while that lady sat in Gus's chair and told us that the situation back in Raleigh had improved.

I watched Bertha's face turn white and felt my stomach do a flip.

Improved?

That lady went on to tell us how Mama was doing better and trying harder and deserved a chance. She explained about how it was always best for children to live with their real parent.

"Whenever possible," she added quickly.

Then she blabbered on and on, but all I heard were words like *Charlie's well-being* and *supervision* and *stable environment*.

Bertha kept pushing at her hair with a shaky hand and nodding, and then that lady said she would send someone to pick me up in a few weeks and that was that.

Believe me when I tell you, my head was spinning. *Why* was I feeling so scared? I sat there on that porch with confusion swirling around me like a swarm of angry bees. Shouldn't I be feeling happy? Hadn't I wanted to go back to Raleigh? Didn't I hate these hillbilly kids here in Colby? Didn't I want to get the heck out of a place where my only friend was an up-down boy and I slept on Cinderella pillowcases in a shabby old house hanging off the side of a mountain?

And then I had a thought that made me jump up and run to the front door, where Bertha was watching that lady's car disappear up the driveway.

"What about Wishbone?" I hollered. "Tell that lady I'm not leaving Wishbone!"

Bertha swiped at her cheeks and pulled me to her and said the perfect Bertha thing.

"I will make things right for you, Charlie," she said. "I promise."

Twenty-Nine

The next day Mama called. Bertha talked to her first, soft and low with her face toward the kitchen wall.

"I know, Carla, but . . ."

". . . think of Charlie . . ."

". . . not fair . . ."

Finally she gave the phone to me.

"Hello?" I said, and felt like a baby. Why couldn't I be strong and sassy-mouthed like Jackie?

Then Mama told me how she can't wait for me to come home and she's been so lonely and nobody understands what she's been going through.

"And Jackie thinks she's so gall-derned grown-up that she's not coming back home and that's fine by me," she said.

After that she started on Scrappy. What a no-good nothing he is and how he left her high and dry.

"Doesn't anybody ever think about me?" she said.

I knew I wasn't really supposed to answer that, so I didn't.

"Scrappy got a tattoo of a blackbird in a cage on the back of his hand," I said.

And guess what happened next?

She hung up!

Click.

Just like that.

"What happened?" Bertha asked.

I shrugged. "I guess she didn't wanna hear about that tattoo."

Bertha stood there slack-jawed, looking from me to the phone and then back at me.

"Maybe y'all just got disconnected," she said. "I bet she'll call back."

So we stood there staring at the phone while the refrigerator hummed and a cat purred beside us.

But the phone didn't ring.

Bertha shook her head. "Nothing ever changes with her," she said. "Carla, Carla, Carla. It's always about Carla."

Then she grabbed me by the shoulders and said, "I'm sorry, Charlie. I shouldn't've said that."

"It's okay."

"No," she said. "No, it isn't. She's your mama."

I wanted to ask Bertha if I really was going back to Raleigh, but I was scared to. Hadn't she said she would make things right? But what did that even mean anyway?

I decided to walk down to the Odoms', hoping my swirling insides would settle down. I clipped Wishbone's leash to his collar and we set off down the road. I let him stop every now and then to sniff a tangle of weeds or inspect a tin can on the side of the road. My swirling stomach didn't settle down until the Odoms' house came into view. Then, just the sight of it set things right again. That weed-filled yard was littered with balls and tools and shoes. Burl's legs stuck out from under his truck in the driveway. Music from a radio drifted out of Mr. Odom's shop in the garage. Cotton was lining up bricks along the edge of the road, and Lenny was swinging a baseball bat at rocks that hit the road sign with a clang. And then there was Howard, working on a crossword puzzle on the steps. By the time I got to the front porch, Mrs. Odom was already out the door giving Wishbone a piece of cheese.

I sat on the steps for a while, not talking, watching Howard working on his puzzle. The thing about Howard was, you could be with him and talk or you could be with him and not talk. He liked you either way.

We went inside to play Monopoly, which I personally think is boring but Howard likes it. Wishbone got mud on the floor but Mrs. Odom didn't even care. She brought us orange Jell-O in coffee mugs and let Cotton jump on the couch.

I kept trying to make myself tell Howard about that squinty-eyed social services lady and how the situation at home had improved. I wanted to put a smile on my face and take a deep breath and say, "Guess what! I'm going back to Raleigh!"

But I just sat there eating orange Jell-O while Howard put another hotel on Boardwalk.

Jackie called that night and told me she couldn't wait to see me again. She told me her new boyfriend, Jake, would take me for a ride on his motorcycle and she could put blue streaks in my hair if I wanted.

"And I'm finally getting my very own apartment, Charlie, so you can have the bedroom all to yourself and—"

"I don't want to go back to Raleigh," I said.

Silence.

"I *said*, I don't want to go back to Raleigh," I hollered.

"How come?"

" 'Cause I want to stay here in Colby."

"But I thought you wanted to come back."

Jackie let out a big, heavy sigh and then she started with I *told* you this and I *told* you that. And what could I do but agree with her? She *had* told me all that. How I had Gus and Bertha treating me like a princess and those good-hearted Odoms thanking the good Lord for me at the supper table. How Howard was the nicest friend I could ever want. How I had these beautiful mountains and that little porch under the stars. I just hadn't *seen* all those things until now. I'd been so busy making my wish that I hadn't seen things the way they really were.

"But Bertha's going to make things right," I told Jackie.

"What does that mean?" she said.

"I'm not sure."

Then she said she'd call again later, and I went to bed with my stomach so tangled up in knots I couldn't sleep. I laid my cheek against Wishbone's warm side and listened to his slow, steady breathing. I couldn't even think about that clothesline of troubles. Shoot, I had so many troubles that line was liable to fall right over.

Thirty

The next day, Mama called again. I could hear her voice clear across the kitchen while she talked to Bertha.

Loud and fast.

Bertha kept saying "Slow down, Carla," and "What're you talking about?"

Then she said, "Wait, what?"

"Chattanooga?"

"With *who*?"

"For how long?"

Bertha kept shaking her head and her face got redder by the minute. Then she hollered, "What about Charlie? You know, your *daughter*?"

Bertha almost never got mad about anything more than a cat bringing a mouse inside, so it was a bit of a shock to hear her yelling like that. But then it got worse. She lit into Mama, telling her how she needed to get a hold of herself and act like a mother. How she needed to think about somebody besides herself sometime.

"So you're just gonna waltz on up to Chattanooga and come back and be a mother when you're good and ready, is that it, Carla?"

And then Bertha was staring at the phone in her hand, and the silence on the other end felt heavy and sad there in that little kitchen.

"Am I going back to Raleigh?" popped out of my mouth when I wasn't even expecting it to.

"No, you aren't," Bertha said.

Then she told me she had some calls to make, and I should go down to Howard's.

I told Howard everything, starting with that squinty-eyed social services lady telling us how the situation in Raleigh had improved and ending with Bertha saying, "No, you aren't."

And when I was done, he said, "Ain't Bertha the best?"

And wasn't that so like Howard, finding the only good part when things are bad? I wondered what he thought about a mama who just waltzes up to Chattanooga instead of making orange Jell-O in coffee mugs.

For a minute, I even wondered if he still wanted to be my friend, knowing my family was all broken up like it was.

But that thought flew right out of my mind when he said, "Let's build a fort."

So we spent the afternoon in the Odoms' dusty, ramshackle garage searching for stuff to make a fort with. Scraps of wood. A warped table with no legs. A rusty stop sign riddled with bullet holes.

Cotton kept following us around saying, "What about this?" and holding up something dumb like a broken hamster cage or an empty paint can. Wishbone like to went crazy sniffing around for mice and chipmunks or whatever else might've been in that garage chewing on bags of bird seed or nesting in a busted radiator.

Lenny and Burl helped us drag everything to the woods at the edge of the yard, and then Howard wanted to sit on the porch and draw a plan for the fort. Me? I'd just dive right in, but not Howard. He was a planner.

We worked on our fort for a while but it was too hot, so we went inside and laid on the living room floor in front of the fan.

I stared up at the water-stained ceiling and said, "I hope I don't have to go back to Raleigh." My voice came out all quivery, and I had to swallow hard to keep the tears from coming.

I hoped Howard wouldn't say, "I thought you *wanted* to go back to Raleigh."

He didn't.

He said, "You're not."

"How do you know?"

"I just know."

He said that so firm and sure that I felt better right away.

After a while, Mrs. Odom came in and told me Bertha had called and that I should go home. So I tied Wishbone's leash to Lenny's bike and headed off up the road with my stomach starting that familiar swirl again.

What if Bertha hadn't been able to make things right for me, after all?

Thirty-One

When I got back, Gus was home from work, sitting in a lawn chair dunking turnip greens in a bucket of water.

"Hey, there, Butterbean," he called out when he saw me.

Wishbone slurped up some of that sandy turnip green water and me and Gus laughed. Bertha's cat named Lula Mae sauntered over and rubbed her head against Wishbone's leg. He gave me a mournful look, but he let her do it.

Later, while Bertha put turnip greens and cornbread and tuna casserole on the table, she told me we would talk about everything after supper.

I didn't know what "talk about everything" meant, so I just said okay. But inside, I felt scared. I pushed tuna casserole around on my plate and didn't say much while

Bertha told us about some friend of hers whose son ran off and joined the army.

"Honest to goodness," she said. "The way she keeps crying and carrying on, you'd think he jumped off a cliff."

After supper, I helped her clear the table and then we went out on the porch to eat peaches with vanilla ice cream. I watched the lightning bugs twinkle down below and waited for us to talk about everything.

Finally Bertha started.

"So, Charlie," she said. "I talked to social services today and told them I didn't think your situation at home has improved, after all. I told them I thought maybe they'd made a mistake."

"You did?"

"I did." Then she told me how they agreed to check on things. She repeated some of those social services kind of words like *reevaluate* and *stable environment*.

"They promised they would get back to me in a few days," Bertha said.

Well, let me tell you, those few days felt like a few years to me. Worry followed me every minute, making my insides flop around and my heart beat like crazy.

Howard kept saying, "Trust me. You're not going back to Raleigh."

But when I asked him how he knew that, he said, "I can't tell you. Just trust me."

I wanted to trust him more than anything, but that ball of worry in my stomach just wouldn't go away. And then, of course, laying in bed with Wishbone snoring beside me, I couldn't stop thinking about how wrong I'd been about everything here in Colby. How I hadn't seen all the good things Jackie saw right away. And then I found myself wanting to be more like Jackie again. And Howard, too. Both of them always seeing the good in things.

I put my head on Wishbone's warm side and made a promise to myself right there in that little room of mine. No matter how things turned out, I was going to try to see the good in things, like Jackie and Howard. I knew I'd probably always have to say "Pineapple" once in a while on account of Scrappy's temper that I have. But, who knows, if I tried hard enough, maybe someday somebody might even call me "good-hearted."

Those few days dragged on and every little thing I looked at nearly turned me into a crying baby, thinking I might be leaving. Bertha stirring grits by the stove with a cat at her feet. Gus out in the garden in his greasy base-ball cap, picking nasty green worms off the tomato plants. Even the shed and the porch and the lawn chairs and the canning jars lined up on that shelf in my room made me sad.

I tried to stay busy at Howard's, but then being at the Odoms' like to broke my heart. That ratty old couch on the porch. The yard full of bicycles and balls and dirty sneakers. And, of course, Howard, studying his fort plans like he was building a castle, then heading out to the edge of the yard with that up-down walk of his.

Finally after a few days, the kitchen phone rang while me and Bertha were out on the porch eating egg salad sandwiches for lunch. She answered it and talked for a while, and when she came back out, the look on her face told me something good was about to happen.

"How would you like to stay here with me and Gus, Charlie?" she said.

My heart nearly leaped right out of my chest. "Stay?" I said.

Bertha nodded. "Stay."

"For how long?"

Then Bertha said almost the exact same words that Jackie had said on her last night in my room. About how

Scrappy was going to keep on being Scrappy and Mama was going to keep on being Mama. And then she told me as long as she had a breath in her body, she was going to make things right for me.

I wanted to jump up and down and pump my fist and let out a cheer that would echo across the valley below us. I wanted to spread my arms like wings and fly right off that porch and out over the treetops and up into the clouds. I wanted to dance with Wishbone and then race down to Howard's to tell him this news.

But what I did first was hug Bertha.

"Yes, ma'am," I said. "I would like to stay with you and Gus." I hugged her one more time and added, "I would like that a lot."

Bertha looked at me all teary-eyed and said, "Guess what I'm doing first thing tomorrow?"

"What?"

"I'm getting every single one of those dang canning jars out of your room."

We laughed and I asked if I could go tell Howard the news.

So me and Wishbone raced down to the Odoms' and up the porch steps. I banged on the screen door hollering, "Guess what, y'all!"

I didn't even wait for anybody to come to the door. I burst right into their living room, which I know was not a very nice thing to do, but I couldn't stop myself.

Howard jumped up from the couch and Mrs. Odom came running in from the kitchen and I said, "I'm staying here! I'm not going back to Raleigh!"

Mrs. Odom hugged me and told me that was the best news ever, but Howard just said, "Told ya."

Then he gave Wishbone half a vanilla wafer and said, "I *knew* you were staying here."

"But how'd you know?" I asked.

"'Cause that was the other part of my wish," he said. "That day at the creek. I wished that you would be my friend and stay here in Colby."

"You did?"

He nodded. "Yep. And since the part about being my friend came true, I knew the other part would, too. But I couldn't tell you 'cause of that rule. You know, that you can't tell your wish to anybody or it won't come true?"

Well, didn't that just beat all, Howard making a wish like that?

On my way home, I thought about how I'd made my wish so many times and it hadn't come true. And there was Howard, getting his wish on the very first try.

Still, my heart felt light as a feather as I turned up the gravel driveway toward Gus and Bertha's.

That night after supper, we sat out on the porch and ate blackberry cobbler and listened to Bertha's stories.

"And *then*," she said, "one time we ran out of gas in the middle of nowhere with three cats in the car. Remember that, Gus?"

He nodded and said, "Yep."

Then Bertha let out a big contented sigh and said, "I never in my wildest dreams would've thought we'd have a family like this, would you, Gus?"

A family like this?

Is that what she'd said?

She *had* said that!

A family.

A *real* family.

A family that cared about me and called me Butterbean and was going to take the canning jars out of my room first thing tomorrow.

A family that wasn't broken.

A family that I'd been wishing for all those times.

I couldn't hardly wait till Sunday, when I could find my flower in the Garden of Blessings and write "My family" on it.

Suddenly Bertha called out, "Star! First star! Everybody make a wish!"

I looked up at that star twinkling over the mountains, but instead of wishing, I just closed my eyes and breathed in the piney air.

My wish had finally come true.

GOFISH

BARBARA O'CONNOR

When did you realize you wanted to be a writer?
I've always loved to write but never dreamed it would be my career. As a child, I wrote stories and poems. My mother kept almost everything, so I have boxes and boxes of my writings. As an adult, I never lost my love of writing, and I adore children. So to combine writing and children is about the best job I can imagine.

What's your favorite childhood memory?
I loved playing in the woods and especially playing in creeks (which shows up in several of my books). I loved catching salamanders, tadpoles, crawfish, and frogs. I once caught a giant bullfrog using an old birdcage—the inspiration for *The Fantastic Secret of Owen Jester*.

As a young person, who did you look up to most?
My dad. He was always the kind of person who would return a lost wallet with all the money inside. He taught me a lot about honesty and doing the right thing.

What was your favorite thing about school?
I loved everything about school. No, really—I did! Especially spelling bees and worksheets.

What were your hobbies as a kid? What are your hobbies now?

I loved to tap dance. I actually still take tap classes occasionally. I loved arts and craft activities, but not so much as an adult. Now I like to garden and walk my dogs. I'm kind of boring that way.

Did you play sports as a kid?

No! I was terrible at sports. I still can't catch a ball to save my life.

What was your "worst" job?

Selling pots and pans door-to-door.

What book is on your nightstand now?

I'm reading *Writing Radar* by Jack Gantos.

Where do you write your books?

I'm very fortunate to have my very own writing studio beside my home in North Carolina. I have silence and privacy. My two dogs like to come spend the day out there with me.

What is your favorite word?

Brouhaha.

What was your favorite book when you were a kid? Do you have a favorite book now?

I loved any books about animals and mysteries. Now, one of my favorite books is *Missing May* by Cynthia Rylant. When I was starting to write for children, I struggled to find my unique writing voice. When I read *Missing May*, I was struck by her strong use of place (the mountains of West Virginia where she grew up). When I began writing stories with a strong sense of place, I found my voice.

What's the best advice you have ever received about writing?

Write the story the way that only you can tell it. Also, don't be afraid to write something that isn't very good. You can make it better. But you can't fix what you haven't written.

Do you ever get writer's block? What do you do to get back on track?

Not often, but when I do, it feels kind of scary. The best way to get back on track, for me, is to read books that inspire me and also to put my draft away for a bit and come back to it with fresh eyes.

What do you want readers to remember about your books?

That I write about characters who behave the way real people do (i.e., they sometimes make mistakes or behave badly). And they live in a less-than-perfect world, the way the real world is.

What do you consider to be your greatest accomplishment?

Raising a son who is empathetic, kind-hearted, honest, and hard-working.

What would your readers be most surprised to learn about you?

I have no sense of smell.

Don't miss a new book from
Barbara O'Connor!

A heartfelt middle grade about a young boy who
goes on an adventure after the loss of his older
brother—timeless, classic, and whimsical.

ONE

The night that Posey and Evalina moved to Harmony, Georgia, Walter Tipple had that dream again.

The one about his birthday.

Mama and Daddy are standing nearby, waiting for him to blow out the candles.

Eleven of them.

Everyone sings "Happy Birthday," but suddenly the screen door bursts open and in steps Walter's brother, Tank, in his army uniform.

He throws his arms out and says, "Look who's back!" while everyone stares, wide-eyed and gape-mouthed, like they've just seen a ghost.

Which, of course, they have.

The candles drip wax onto the buttercream frosting that Mama makes so good.

And then it happens.

Every single time Walter has that dream.

The ghost that is Tank takes off his army hat, plunks it down on Walter's head, and says, "Blow out them candles, little man, and I'll show you my world." He slaps Walter on the back and adds, "But you gotta blow 'em *all* out. First try. No cheating."

He grins that grin of his with the chipped front tooth.

Then he crosses his arms and taps his foot and says, "I ain't got all day."

So Walter looks down at those eleven candles, takes a deep breath . . .

. . . and wakes up.

Every single time.

The night that Evalina and Posey moved to Harmony, Walter had sat on the edge of the bed after that dream with his heart racing.

Then he'd heard a car bouncing and squeaking up the gravel road toward Ernest and Nadine's old tumbledown house next door.

He got out of bed and padded to the window, the

wide plank floor cool under his bare feet. The full moon glowed over the yard, making the clothesline cast an eerie shadow, like a long black snake that slithered through the garden and over the lawn chair where Daddy sometimes napped in the afternoon.

By the light of the moon, Walter saw Evalina's car pulling a trailer piled high with cardboard boxes. A washing machine. A mattress.

He hadn't seen Posey or her scruffy little dog, Pork-chop, sitting in the front seat beside Evalina.

But the next day, he had done what Mama asked him to and run up to that old house with a jar of her bread-and-butter pickles. He stood on the wooden porch with half the boards missing and started counting to ten to calm his nerves before knocking on the door. But he had only gotten to six when a skinny, scabby-kneed girl came busting out onto the porch, followed by a small, yap-ping dog.

"Can't you read?" the girl hollered.

Walter nearly fell backward into the prickly bushes along the porch. And just when he thought his beating heart might come to a screeching halt, that girl stuck her face up close to his and said, "I suppose you can't talk, neither."

"Um . . ." Walter said, looking down at the pickle jar.

"Stick out your tongue," the girl snapped.

So, of course, that is exactly what Walter did.

He stuck out his tongue.

That was when Evalina came out onto the porch and said, "Good gravy and green beans, Posey. What you doing to that boy?"

"Checking to see if he can hear me, 'cause he sure can't read." Posey jabbed a finger at the sign nailed on the porch railing:

NO SOLICITORS

That sign had been there as long as Walter could remember and he *still* didn't know what solicitors were. He'd always figured it meant any human being who was breathing because Ernest and Nadine hadn't wanted *anybody* to set foot on their property. They stayed inside that falling-down house the livelong day, only opening the door every now and then to shoo cats out of their weed-filled yard.

Then one day Nadine died and three days later Ernest died. Not long after that, Mama heard somebody at the post office say that their daughter from Tennessee was coming to live in their old house.

Evalina.

Mama hadn't heard that Evalina had a skinny, scabby-kneed daughter named Posey and a yapping little dog named Porkchop.

Which was why it had come as a bit of a shock to Walter to find himself on their porch with a jar of pickles and that girl glaring at him and her dog snapping and snarling.

After he got over the shock, he took a good hard look at Posey and felt his spirits lift a little.

Right there in the middle of Posey's left cheek was a large heart-shaped birthmark.

Deep dark brown against her pale, freckled skin.

The instant Walter saw that birthmark, he began to think that maybe he and Posey were destined to be kindred spirits, bound together by the misfortune of being an easy target.

Walter had a lifetime of experience in being an easy target.

He was a quiet, timid, pigeon-toed boy with a lazy eye that never seemed to want to look where the other eye was looking.

Such boys were easy targets for the sharp-tongued kids in Harmony.

Now here was this girl with a heart-shaped birthmark on her cheek who was surely going to be an easy target, too.

Walter had waited his whole life for a kindred spirit and now here she was.

True, she seemed a little wild, wagging her finger at him and going on about that sign on the porch railing.

But then, Walter figured, beggars can't be choosers when it comes to kindred spirits.

He handed Evalina the jar of pickles, and that little dog snarled and snapped at his ankles, making him jump down off the porch, landing in the red dirt yard with a *thud*.

"Hush up, Porkchop," Posey said, holding the dog by his collar. She peered down at Walter and said, "He only bites if I tell him to."

Walter looked up at the dog and felt his mouth drop open in surprise.

That scruffy little dog only had three legs!

Two in the front and one in the back.

Posey must've seen Walter's surprise, because she said, "You gotta be tough when you look like ol' Porkchop here. He's a scrapper." She jabbed a thumb at herself and added, "Like me."

When he headed back home that day, Walter felt a little lighter. Maybe this summer was going to get better. The Tipples lived so far from town that Walter had never had anyone but Tank to hang out with. Now that Tank was gone, he spent every day alone.

His mind whirled with images of him and Posey having a grand old time together.

Looking for salamanders under the rotten logs down by the river.

Maybe adding a second story to the fort he and Tank had built way back in the woods behind a pile of termite-riddled lumber that used to be somebody's barn.

But later that night, Walter felt that familiar Mr. Doubt come creeping back, turning him into his worry-filled self again. He thought about Posey pointing at that NO SOLICITORS sign and squinting right up in his face so bossy and all.

He was starting to realize that Posey was probably one of those kids who had perfected the fine art of bully-thwarting.

He'd bet anything that when summer was over, she'd march herself right into Harmony Elementary School and dare those kids to laugh at her just by sending them a glare as mighty as any laser.

She'd probably snatch fish sticks right off the plates of first-graders at lunch or dare the third-graders to touch her birthmark and then charge them a quarter if they did.

Yep. Posey was a bully-thwarter the way that he, Walter Tipple, could never be.

She and that dog, Porkchop, were tough, the way that he, Walter Tipple, would never be.

By the time he fell asleep that night, Mr. Doubt had stepped aside and Mr. Disappointment had settled in. A bully-thwarter like Posey wouldn't want to hang out with a loser like him.

But then, the very next day, something happened that told Walter that fate might finally be on his side, sending him the kindred spirit he'd been waiting for, after all.

Because the very next day, when he and Posey and Porkchop were pushing their way through tangled pricker bushes and climbing over fallen trees in the dense woods beside the river, they found a dead man.

BARBARA O'CONNOR was born and raised in Greenville, South Carolina. She has written many critically acclaimed books for children, including *How to Steal a Dog* and *The Fantastic Secret of Owen Jester*. She now lives in Duxbury, Massachusetts, a historic seaside village not far from Plymouth Rock.

barbaraoconnor.com